THE OVER-THE-HILL GHOST

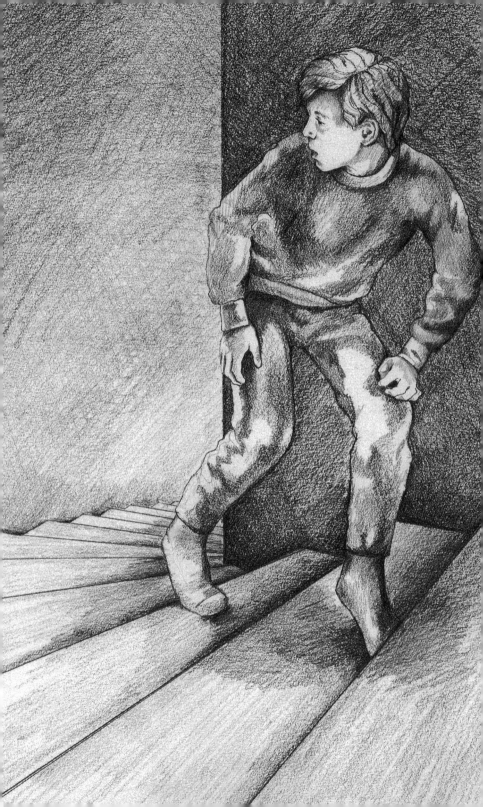

The Over-the-Hill GHOST

By Ruth Calif
Illustrated by Joan Holub

Pelican Publishing Company
GRETNA 1988

Library of Congress Cataloging-in-Publication Data

Calif, Ruth
   The-over-the-hill ghost / by Ruth Calif: illustrated by Joan
Holub
   p. cm.
   Summary: A young boy, hardened by life in a big city, is taught
respect for human values by an aging ghost whom he helps solve a
long-ago murder, recovering a hidden cache of money in the process.
   ISBN 0-088289-667-9
   [1. Ghosts—Fiction. 2. Mystery and detective stories.]
I. Holub, Joan, ill. II. Title
PZ7.C12860v 1988
[Fic.]—dc19   87-30523

Manufactured in the United States of America
Published by Pelican Publishing Company, Inc.
1101 Monroe Street, Gretna, Louisiana 70053

To my son
Gary Lee Calif
with love

CONTENTS

THE OVER-THE-HILL GHOST

CHAPTER ONE

JAMIE MAKES A FRIEND

"Here, Fireplug!" Jamie called, flopping on the grass under a big oak tree.

He watched the shaggy dog race toward him, then fell back laughing when the little animal jumped on his chest and licked his nose with a sloppy red tongue. Soon he pushed Fireplug off and sat up, frowning.

"Wish we were back in New York," he muttered. "What's there to do here in the sticks?"

The dog whimpered, small brown eyes open wide. Jamie's arm went around him.

"I'm glad you're here," he said. "I hate this dumb old farm!"

The fresh spring breeze rustled the leaves overhead while Jamie's wistful gaze swept across the adjacent countryside. Neat posts and barbed wire separated the fields around him. To his citified eyes, the small fenced plots looked huge.

He saw the boy and the big red dog at the same moment Fireplug spotted them. Fireplug's ears pricked up while a low growl sounded in his throat. He broke from Jamie's grasp and rushed toward the oncoming pair.

"Fireplug!" Jamie called. He rose quickly. "Fireplug, you get back here!"

Disregarding the warning, the dog ran on. Jamie followed, still shouting after him. When Fireplug reached the bigger animal, he threw himself at the red throat. Curly tan hair mixed with shiny red while the dogs snarled and snapped at each other.

The strange boy's cries added to the din. "O'Brien! Come!" And to Jamie he shouted, "Get your dog! Pull him out of there!"

Jamie tried to grab the small rear end, but Fireplug slipped from his hands. The other boy's arms went around the red dog, but when the animal lunged forward he lost his grip.

"O'Brien! Hold!" the boy ordered.

The red dog pinned Fireplug to the ground with a big paw placed firmly on his chest. Try as he would, Fireplug could not free himself. He wriggled and struggled under the bigger dog's paw and tried to bite him, but the effort was futile.

Jamie rushed in and pulled Fireplug away from the bared teeth and angry growls. The other boy grabbed the collar on his dog and pulled him backward.

"Now sit!" the other boy ordered. He ran his hands over the big neck and smoothed the hair on the broad back, then looked over at Jamie.

"Is your dog okay?"

Jamie held onto Fireplug, trying to see if he had been

hurt, but the squirming dog was hard to control. Soon the growls changed to panting. A rumble of warning now and then came from deep inside the tan throat.

"He's okay, I guess, and lucky for you!" Jamie said. "Nobody hurts my dog, 'less they want to tangle with me."

"Well, your dog started the fight. O'Brien would have killed him if he'd been by himself. Why did your dog come at him like that?"

Jamie thought about it. "Well, Fireplug's a fighter and he doesn't care how big the other guy is. So I guess he tackled your dog just 'cause he was there."

"That's a dumb reason to fight."

"Oh, yeah?" Jamie glared at the other boy. "He could lick any dog in our neighborhood! He'd show the new dogs who was boss right away." He looked at the other dog. " 'Course, Fireplug never saw one as big as yours before."

"Where you from?"

"New York."

"What's your name?"

"Jamie. Jamie Boyd. But, pretty soon I want people to call me Jim. I'm twelve years old." He looked at the other boy and asked "Who are you?"

"I'm Scooter Johnson and I'm thirteen. My real name is Sylvester, but *nobody* better call me that!" He patted the red dog and added, "This is O'Brien of County Cork. He's a registered Irish Setter."

Jamie ran his hand over the panting Fireplug. "What's registered mean?" he asked.

"That means he's purebred—sort of like royalty. He has lots of champions in his background."

"So does Fireplug; only nobody ever wrote down their

names."

Scooter nodded. "I can tell he's a good dog. Your folks buy the old Mathieson place?"

"Yeah," Jamie said, pushing a strand of brown hair out of his eyes. "We moved in last week. It sure is different out here. Ain't nothin' to do."

"Sure there is." Scooter loosened his grasp on the setter's collar. "Tomorrow there's an Easter-egg hunt at the church. You going?"

A look of scorn crossed Jamie's face. "That's for little kids! Don't tell me you still think there's an Easter bunny and dumb stuff like that!"

Scooter shook his tow-colored head and his freckled face crinkled as he grinned. "No, 'course not. It's for the little kids mostly, but I still like hard-boiled eggs and candy. Don't you?"

"Yeah, I guess." Jamie looked from Fireplug to O'Brien. "Your dog sure minds good."

"He didn't come when I told him to, but he's never had another dog hanging onto his throat, so I guess that doesn't count. He's been to obedience school."

"That figures," Jamie said darkly. "Monday I start school, and a bus is coming to get me, so there's no way I can cut."

"School's not so bad." Scooter walked over and sat beside Jamie and Fireplug. "Reckon your dog would let me pet him?"

"Sure. Fireplug, this is Scooter." Jamie chuckled. "He's never been whipped before, so his feelings might be hurt."

Scooter held out the back of his hand for Fireplug to sniff. After the little dog touched it with his nose, Scooter turned his palm upward. Then he gently scratched

Fireplug just behind one ear.

"O'Brien didn't really whip him, Jamie. Your dog just surprised him at first. He had to hold Fireplug down so your dog wouldn't tear him to pieces. Say, how come you call him that, anyway?"

Jamie's smile turned sheepish. "I was just a little kid when I got him. I gave him that name 'cause he'd always head straight for a fireplug when we came out of the house." He sighed. "There ain't even any of them around here."

"We have a volunteer fire department that brings a water truck and pump when there's a fire," Scooter said. "I plan to be a fireman when I'm old enough. Pa says that house your folks bought is a real firetrap, Jamie."

" 'Bout like the tenements in the city," Jamie agreed. "Every so often one of them goes up in smoke, but it's usually because somebody sets it off. Our house sure is a big old place. You been in it?"

"No. The Mathiesons didn't have any kids. After they were killed, folks came out digging around to look for the money the old man buried, but nobody ever found it. They said there were ghosts out here. Pa said the farm was willed to a cousin in New York, and he never even came here to see it."

Jamie nodded. "Guess that's who Dad bought it from. After the cops busted me, Dad said it was time us kids lived somewhere besides an apartment in the city. He's a writer, so he can live anywhere."

Scooter's mouth dropped open at Jamie's words, and he closed it with a snap. "You been *arrested*?" he asked. "What for?"

A shrug lifted Jamie's shoulders. "Sure, I've been

busted," he bragged. "Who hasn't? The gang dared me
to rip off a new ball when ours went down a sewer, so
I did. Only it made a bump under my sweater and the
cops caught me."

"Did they send you to *jail*?"

"Nah, dummy. Juveniles don't go to jail. I got a lecture from a judge and another from Dad, but that was
all. Only now we're living on a farm, and I can't hang
out with my gang." His voice was glum. "I even have to
take care of a bunch of dumb old chickens, unless I can
get dumb old Margaret to do it."

"Who's Margaret?"

"My sister. You got any brothers and sisters?"

Scooter shook his head. "Wish I did. Big families have
lots of fun."

"A sister ain't no fun. She's only a year older than me,
but she's real bossy. 'Do this, do that'—and if I don't,
she rats on me. I tried to get the eggs yesterday, but hens
peck. The old rooster jumped on Fireplug's back and flapped his wings against him all the way across the bar-
nyard." He glanced down at his dog and patted the curly
head. "You wish you were back in the city, don't you,
boy?" Fireplug raised his head and licked Jamie's chin.

"I've been to New York lots of times," Scooter said.
"Pa takes me with him when he goes. It sure doesn't look
like much fun to me. Houses all jammed together and no
place to play. Why would you want to go back?"

"There's lots of places to play," Jamie answered. "We
play kick-the-can in the street and watch-for-muggers in
the alleys."

"Muggers?"

Jamie laughed. "Yeah. The big guys snatch purses

and run to hide in the alleys. If they catch us, they beat up on us, but I can outrun any of 'em."

"It doesn't sound like much fun," Scooter said. "Out here we go on hayrides and weiner roasts and stuff like that. You coming to the egg hunt tomorrow?"

"Probably." Jamie let go of Fireplug when he got up. "Mom says I have to go to Sunday school, so I'll most likely hang around after."

Fireplug walked stiffly over to O'Brien and the dogs looked at each other. O'Brien rose, his tail waving. The raised hair on Fireplug's neck lowered. His short tail flicked back and forth, then broke into a friendly wag. He raised his nose to O'Brien's for a sniff before he trotted back to Jamie.

"They like each other," Scooter said. "You want to come home with me for some cookies?"

"Can't today. I have to collect eggs before the sun sets, Mom said, so guess I'd better go do it. Come over to our place anytime you want. Maybe tomorrow after the egg hunt? Or is the *Easter bunny* gonna be at your house?" Jamie snickered.

Scooter stiffened. "We gonna have to fight, too, before we can be friends?"

"Hey, . . I was only kidding," Jamie answered. "I know you know there ain't no big rabbit throwing eggs around on Easter."

"Well, don't tell the little kids tomorrow. It's kind of fun for them to still think there's an Easter bunny and ghosts and stuff. Didn't you like to when you were little?"

Jamie shook his head. "My Mom told me a long time ago there wasn't anything like that."

"You might change your mind, now you're living

in the old Mathieson house. Somebody killed the Mathiesons trying to get them to tell where their money was buried. Folks say your house has been haunted since then."

Jamie laughed, then flapped his arms and hooted like an owl. He stopped when something Scooter said came to mind.

"How much money?" he asked.

Scooter shrugged. "Pa said people figure old Mathieson had at least ten thousand dollars. He sold some property over in the next county and never put the money in a bank, at least so far as anybody knew. Everybody figures it's buried somewhere. The sheriff is still trying to find out who killed the Mathiesons, but most likely it was tramps who did it."

"That's a lot of money," Jamie said slowly. "Maybe I'll find it."

"People stopped coming out to look for it after they got scared off a few times," Scooter said. "They say a ghost is guarding it."

"Pooh! There ain't no ghosts," Jamie said.

Scooter shifted from one foot to the other. "Maybe not . . . but old houses have funny noises and stuff. People always say empty places are haunted."

"That's dumb! 'Bout half the tenements in the city are empty, and there's no ghosts there—only winos and dopers. They're the ones who set the places on fire. Themselves, too, sometimes."

"Why?" Scooter asked.

Jamie shrugged. "Sometimes the owners can collect insurance, but mostly the winos are trying to get warm by building a fire," he answered.

Scooter nodded.

"I haven't been up in our attic yet," Jamie said. "Dad decided we'd only use the two bottom floors so it'd be easier to keep warm." Jamie watched Scooter as he added slyly, "The third floor and attic are where the ghosts probably hang out. When you come over, we'll go up and meet 'em." He hunched his shoulders and covered his snicker with his hand.

Scooter scowled, then replaced the frown with a grin. "Okay. I ain't afraid of 'em if they're there."

He glanced at the setter. "Heel, O'Brien!" he commanded. Scooter's smile grew wider when the big dog rose and stood at his side. "See you later, Jamie."

Jamie watched the two walk away, then looked down at Fireplug. "Heel," he said, aping Scooter. He laughed when Fireplug jumped up to paw his leg. "Watch it, boy, or you'll have to go to school, too."

He walked toward home while Fireplug ran in wide circles around him, sniffing the bushes and rocks. "Ghosts!" Jamie snickered to himself, shaking his head. Scooter sure was dumb if he believed in junk like that, but he was the first boy Jamie had met since his family's move to the country. A guy needed buddies.

But, ten thousand dollars; now *that* was another matter. Money was something Jamie *could* believe in because it was real. And *ten thousand dollars* . . . wow! He walked faster in a beeline for home.

CHAPTER TWO

THE GHOST APPEARS

When the old house came in sight, Jamie stopped to look at it. The building rose gaunt against the sky to four stories. It had once been white, but now only spots of dirty paint remained. The top floor was cut by a sloping roof and gables with blank-eyed windows. A brick chimney on one side and a larger brick chimney at the back pointed skyward.

The rays of the setting sun caught one of the panes of glass and flashed light into Jamie's face. He blinked and raised a hand to shield his eyes.

"Firetrap," he muttered. "If the spooks around here are as shabby as the house, they'd be over-the-hill for sure; at least in the scare department," Jamie chuckled to himself.

A wide veranda stretched across the front of the building with three steps leading up from the ground. One of the steps had a rotten spot in the middle where everybody walked, but Dad had nailed a new board across it when they moved in.

It sure wasn't like the little apartment they had in New York. Here the rooms were big, with high ceilings and tall, skinny windows, instead of small and cozy. The only thing better was now he had a room of his own. In the city he'd slept on a couch in the dining room so Margaret could have the den.

Behind the old farmhouse was a big crumbling barn. From where he stood Jamie could only see one side of it, which was enough so far as he was concerned. Another thing Dad had done was to buy a bunch of hens and put them in the barn. A rooster, too, so they could raise chickens.

Jamie glanced down at Fireplug. "Better not tackle that old rooster again, boy," he warned. "Things are different out here."

He moved forward, thinking about how he could get the eggs out from under the hens without getting pecked. The sun was going down fast, so he knew he'd better hurry.

Then a car turned off the narrow road in front of the house and parked in the drive.

"Oh, no," Jamie groaned. "What'd I do now?"

The car had a red bulb on its roof and the word "SHERIFF" lettered across the door. Every time a police car had parked in front of the apartment in New York, Jamie knew he was in for some kind of lecture.

"Lousy cops!" he muttered angrily. "Come here, Fireplug, before you get a ticket for walking on the grass."

Fireplug had wandered off to sniff new ground, but now he ran back to stay beside Jamie while they slowly approached the house.

"I haven't been here long enough to get into trouble," Jamie reasoned to himself. "I haven't gone anywhere except here around the farm. Wonder what's up?"

By the time Jamie reached the front yard, a lanky man in a khaki uniform had gotten out of the police car and was talking to Jamie's father. He looked around.

"This your son, Mr. Boyd?"

Jamie's father motioned him over. "This is Jamie, Sheriff Griffith. I'm sure he'll never give you any trouble." His glance at Jamie promised more than a lecture if he did.

"Hello," Jamie said.

The sheriff smiled. "Now why would a smart young fellow like this give me trouble? I'm glad to meet you, young man. I make honorary deputies out of all the youngsters in the county so they'll help me keep the peace. Here, I'll give you a badge." He felt in his pockets, then shook his head. "Guess I forgot to bring one, Jamie. I'll bring it next time I'm out this way."

Jamie nodded, keeping a deadpan face. Wouldn't the old gang crack up if he became a *deputy*? This hick cop was a riot!

"I was just telling your father to watch out for treasure hunters," the sheriff continued. "Folks still think there's money buried out here, although the weird goings-on scared them off before you folks moved in. Now there are people living here, they might get brave enough to come snooping around. I put up a NO TRESPASSING sign, but somebody stole it."

"I hear the Mathiesons were murdered," Jim Boyd said.

"Only the old man," Sheriff Griffith said. "According to the coroner, Mrs. Mathieson died of a heart attack. I guess seeing her husband dead was too much for her. They were both in their eighties."

"How was Mr. Mathieson killed?" Jamie's father asked.

The sheriff glanced at Jamie. "Maybe I'd better not say, Mr. Boyd. Don't want to give your son nightmares."

Jamie's father glanced at him. "I'm afraid Jamie's already seen worse than anything that has happened here."

"Well . . Mathieson was stabbed," the sheriff said. "The knife went in pretty deep; that is, if it *was* a knife. The coroner's report said death resulted from a wound inflicted by a sharp instrument."

"The weapon was never found?"

Sheriff Griffith shook his head. "No, and I haven't solved who did it—much as I wish I could. Don't like to think of a killer walking around loose." He put out his hand. "Well, I wanted to meet you, Mr. Boyd, and warn you about prowlers so you won't shoot anybody. They're mostly harmless. Maybe your dog will keep them away, although he's pretty small."

"He's plenty tough," Jamie said.

The sheriff grinned at him. "I just bet he is," he said. Then his smile vanished. "The Mathiesons had a watchdog, but he disappeared about a week before the tragedy. Mr. Mathieson came in to ask if I'd seen him anywhere." He shook his head. "That dog wasn't one you'd overlook, that's for sure. He was big and hairy and ugly as a mud fence. And mean." He shook his head as he thought about the dog. "Well, I've got to go. See you later, Mr. Boyd,

Jamie." With a friendly nod, he climbed into the police car and drove away.

Jamie's glance locked with his father's. "See? It wasn't about me this time, Dad."

"And it better not ever be, Jamie."

"Aw, Dad . . ."

"I mean it, Jamie. You're starting new here in the country, away from that crazy gang of yours. You'd better keep your nose clean."

"I have to gather eggs," Jamie said quickly. His father was building up to a lecture, and that was something he could do without. Before more could be said, Jamie ran around to the back of the house and in through the kitchen door. Fireplug raced in between Jamie's feet.

"Hi, Mom. Can I have somethin' to eat?" Jamie asked.

"Too close to suppertime," his mother answered. "Here's the egg basket." She smiled at Jamie, then frowned at Fireplug when he jumped up on a chair. "Down!" she ordered.

Ellen Boyd was a small woman with hair the same dark brown as Jamie's. Her eyes were as blue as her son's, only more serious. Her smile returned when Fireplug jumped down.

"Dogs don't belong on the furniture," she said. "Now go get the eggs and fill the feeder and waterer, Jamie. We'll eat when you're through in the barn."

Jamie picked up the basket. "They peck when I try to get the eggs," he grumbled.

"They're just chickens, Jamie. You aren't afraid of them, are you?"

"I'm not afraid of anything," Jamie answered. "It's just that getting pecked hurts."

"Well, I've seen you roughhouse with Fireplug, and I *know* chickens would never be that hard on you. Hens can't harm you—you just think you'll be hurt and then you are. Go on, go do your chores."

From her tone Jamie knew he'd better do as he was told. He carried the basket out the door with Fireplug trailing behind. The closer they came to the barn, the more Jamie's feet dragged, but there was no help for it; he'd have to get those darned eggs.

The barn walls had boards missing here and there, allowing the breeze to blow through with funny swooshing sounds. Moldy stacks of hay were scattered around a loft overhead. Pieces of it were apt to tumble through the holes and down the back of Jamie's neck, and they itched like blazes until he got them out.

Shadows hid the corners of the barn, and Fireplug sniffed at them before he followed Jamie. Jamie looked around and saw that the hens had mostly gone to roost for the night.

"Hens can't harm you," he said in a high-pitched voice that sarcastically mimicked his mother's. "Especially if they've gone to bed," he added. "Fireplug, you'd better wait outside."

The dog's shaggy head rose at the sound of his name, but he stayed at Jamie's heels. The old rooster stirred, eyeing Jamie and Fireplug from the highest rung of the chicken roost.

Jamie carried a bucket to the well outside. The well was constructed from rocks placed together in a circle with a wide open top. A bucket on a windlass had to be lowered to the water and then raised with a hand crank. Jamie filled the bucket to the top. Slopping water with each step, he carried it to the metal waterer inside the barn. The lid had to be pulled off and the water dumped inside, then the cover had to be put back on. Somehow or other this allowed the water to fill the narrow trough around the bottom to just below the rim. Jamie wondered how the water knew when to stop rising, but he hadn't figured out the answer yet.

An old grain bin inside the barn held the sack of feed. Jim Boyd had knocked out several of the horse stalls to make room for the chickens, but at the time he said the bin would be handy to store things where the chickens couldn't reach them. For that reason he had left it intact.

Jamie opened the bin door and realized it was so dark inside he'd have to feel his way to find the gallon can and fill it from the sack. His fingers touched the edge of the can and he managed to scoop it full of the grain. He carried it to the metal feeder and poured the grain evenly down the length of the trough, then replaced the can in the grain bin and closed the door.

There was nothing more to do but collect the eggs. He picked up the basket and walked to the nests. Fireplug was still with him, which somehow helped. One of the hens had flown at Jamie from a nest the day before, and the flapping of her wings against his face scared him.

Through the missing boards Jamie could see twilight outside. The shadows in the corners had spread through the old barn. In the dim light, he peered into the dark nests and discovered to his joy that the first ones were empty. Hey, this was all right! From now on he would wait until the old hens went to bed before he gathered eggs. He went from nest to nest, transferring the smooth ovals from their straw beds into the basket.

Then he reached into a dark hole and felt feathers. Before he could withdraw his hand, a hard beak pecked the back of it. Jamie jerked away, a sharp pain throbbing from the spot. One of the hens was still there, probably trying to hatch her eggs. Dad gave instructions for Jamie to take all the eggs for now. Others would be left to hatch later on, when they were ready to raise little chickens.

"Dumb old hen," Jamie muttered angrily. "Get off that nest!"

The hen clucked in anger, ruffling her feathers to cover and protect the eggs beneath her. The old rooster answered her from his perch with a sort of gurgling in his throat. Fireplug growled.

Jamie tried to slip his hand under the hen, but a series of rapid pecks made him pull it back.

Suddenly the air inside the barn turned chilly. A gust of icy wind hit the back of Jamie's neck, causing him to shiver.

"Lift the hen out of the nest, boy," a voice behind him said.

Jamie turned and saw a thin old man with wild gray hair and a long beard to match.

"Reach for her with both hands, and while she's deciding which one to peck, you can lift her out and put her on the roost," the old man continued.

Fireplug whined. The hair on his neck bristled and stood on end. Instead of charging, however, he took several steps backward.

"Who're you?" Jamie demanded.

"My name's Elmer," the old man answered. "Your name's Jamie, isn't it?"

"How'd you know that? Where'd you come from?"
Jamie's frightened voice quivered.

"Take it easy, young man," Elmer said in a soft,
reassuring voice. "There's no need to be afraid of me. I
live around here."

"Where?" Jamie asked, still uncertain about what he
was seeing.

The old man scratched his head. "Oh . . around," he
answered evasively.

Fireplug whimpered. Jamie pulled the collar of his shirt
tighter around his neck and shivered again. He glanced
at his dog and saw him standing, as though frozen, tail
pointed straight up.

"Whatsa matter, boy?" Jamie asked, looking from his
dog to the old man, then back to Fireplug. "You *scared?*"
Fireplug was never afraid of anything until now.

Fireplug tucked his tail under his body and made for
the door. The movement drew the rooster's attention.
With a squawk, he flew from the perch in a beeline for
Fireplug's back.

Elmer waved his arms. The rooster stopped in mid air,
wings flapping while he tried to keep from falling. He
landed in a heap on the straw-covered floor just as
Fireplug made his escape through the door. Jamie laughed
when the big bird regained his balance and stalked back
to the perch. The icy tension that had hung in the air since
the appearance of this strange old man was broken.

"You saved Fireplug, Elmer," Jamie said, as a sense
of trust began to build up in him. He then turned to the
nest he was having trouble with, and made a face at the
hen roosting on it.

"Go on, Jamie, lift her out," Elmer urged.

Gently placing the basket on the floor, Jamie stuck both hands inside the nest and grasped the feathered bundle. Sure enough, the hen squawked in anger but no sharp beak attacked him. He lifted her out of the nest and placed her on the lowest rung of the roost.

"Now get your eggs before she flies back to look for them," Elmer said.

Jamie returned to his task, delicately placing eggs on top of eggs in the basket until he reached the last nest. He noticed the air in the barn getting warmer again, so he smoothed his collar down where it belonged.

"Guess that's all," he said, turning to where Elmer had stood. A surprised look crossed his face. "Hey, Elmer . . . where'd you go?"

There was no answer and no sound except the sleepy chirps of the chickens as they settled down for the night. A finger of something akin to fear poked at Jamie's stomach.

CHAPTER THREE

HIDDEN TREASURE?

The old man had vanished! Jamie looked everywhere, even into the darkest corners of the barn. Where could Elmer have disappeared to so quickly? Jamie brushed aside the queer feeling that had come over him and picked up the basket of eggs. He was hungry.

Inside the kitchen Fireplug was cowering under a chair. When Jamie looked his way, the dog whined.

"What's wrong with Fireplug?" Jamie's mother asked. "He's been acting scared ever since he clawed his way in here." She pointed at a ragged hole in the screen door. "Look what he did!"

"That dog is a pest," Jamie's sister Margaret complained. "He wrecked the door just like he tore up my shoe. Why don't we get rid of him?"

Jamie glared at her. "He wouldn't have gotten hold of your shoe if you'd put it in the closet where it belongs. He's played with old shoes ever since he was a pup, so

how do you expect him to know when one's new?"

"All right, you two," their mother said. "Margaret, go tell your father supper is ready. Jamie, I'll take the eggs. Now, tell me; what scared your dog?"

The damage to the screen door made Jamie uncomfortable. His mother had warned him that if Fireplug didn't stop tearing things up, the dog would have to be kept outside.

"An old man out in the barn scared him, Mom. Him and the rooster. That old bird went after Fireplug again."

"What old man, Jamie?"

"Oh, just some guy said his name was Elmer. He looked sort of weird, I guess, and Fireplug took off. The old man kept the rooster from landing on Fireplug's back again."

"What old man?" Jamie's father asked, entering alongside Margaret. "One of the neighbors come around?"

"He said he lived around here, but he didn't say where, Dad."

"Where is he now?"

"He took off while I was getting the eggs."

"I hope there are no tramps coming around to sleep in that barn," his father said. "One spark could set the whole thing up in flames."

Jim Boyd had a worried frown on his face as he talked. Jamie wondered if it was because of the old man or was he still thinking of the trouble with the police in New York. Dad was furious when he had to take Jamie to juvenile court, but grown-ups didn't know how rough it was to be a kid in a gang. You *had* to be tougher than the rest or be bullied around and beat up on.

His father had begun looking older since Jamie got busted. Gray hairs started appearing in the dark brown almost overnight. He had always stood tall to show off his six-foot body, but now his shoulders sort of slumped at times. Did all dads get old that fast?

Fireplug let out a sudden yelp, and fled from under the table when they sat down to eat. Margaret looked smug.

"You kicked him!" Jamie shouted accusingly.

"Well, I don't see why we have to fall over your stupid dog every time we move," Margaret said. "Dogs belong outside anyway."

"Not this one!" Jamie said. "He's slept with me since he was a pup, and nobody's gonna boot him out now!"

"Stop bickering, you two," Jamie's mother warned. "The dinner table is only for pleasant conversation." Ellen glanced at her husband before she continued. "Perhaps you should keep Fireplug outside except at night when you take him into your room, Jamie."

"Then I'll stay out too, dammit!" Jamie muttered.

"That's it, young man!" his father broke in, an angry scowl crossing his face. "For that remark, you can go to bed without the rest of your dinner. If your behavior doesn't improve here, your next move will be to a military school, and dogs aren't allowed there at all."

Jamie held back further angry words. Staying in some dumb old school where Fireplug couldn't be with him was something he'd rather not think about. Maybe he had better shape up a little, after all.

He put down his napkin and rose from the table. "Sorry, Dad . . . Mom. I'll fix the screen door tomorrow."

His father's scowling face nodded in the direction of Jamie's room, and Jamie obediently walked toward the front hall. He didn't mind telling his parents he was sorry, but he would be fried before he'd give in to dumb old Margaret.

"I'll be up in a little while," his mother called after him. Out in the hall Jamie broke into a run. He raced up the staircase to the second floor with Fireplug at his heels. His room was at the far end of the upper hallway, and when they were inside, Jamie closed the door.

"Dumb old girls always cause trouble, boy," he said, petting the shaggy ears. "Don't let it bother you."

Jamie reached into his pocket and brought out a big chunk of steak. He flopped backward on the bed and grunted when Fireplug jumped up on his stomach. The dog slid off after nosing the meat. Jamie broke off a piece of steak for his dog, then one for himself, and the two ate contentedly until it was gone.

"Pretty good, hey, boy?" Jamie sat stroking his dog. "When you've been sent to bed without supper as often as we have you learn to plan for it. Right?"

Fireplug raised his head and licked Jamie's nose.

"Cut it out!" Jamie said, as he dried the wet spot Fireplug's tongue left on his nose. Jamie started to unbutton his shirt, and just as he did a shiver rippled through him. The air had suddenly grown chilly. "Better get my pajamas on before Mom gets here, Fireplug. We're supposed to be in bed."

He pulled the cord on the bedside lamp and the room lit up. With a startled, terrified yelp, Fireplug dived under the covers. Jamie sat up staring around the room, his mouth open.

Elmer was seated in an easy chair near the wall. His grin was sheepish. "Hi, Jamie," he said nonchalantly.

"What are you doing here?" Jamie demanded.

"Oh . . I just thought I'd sit here a while. I've had this whole house to myself for a long time until you folks came, and it's been lonely."

"You mean you've been living *here*?"

The gray head nodded. "Well, not in this room exactly, but around the house. Sometimes in the barn. This is a gloomy old place when it's empty."

The old man wore a shabby gray suit. His shoes were scuffed and run down at the heels. One sole had a big hole in it and a dirty sock showed through.

A groan came from his wrinkled lips when Elmer shifted in the chair. "Sure is cold at night. Makes my arthritis act up like it does when there's a storm coming."

"Well, gee . . ." Jamie didn't know what to say, but then an idea came to him. "You had supper?"

"I don't eat, but thanks, anyhow."

"You don't *eat*? Ever?"

The old man shook his head.

There was a knock on the door and then Jamie's mother came in. "You're not in your pajamas yet, Jamie. Come on, get moving," she said.

Jamie said nothing, and his mother shivered. "It's cold in here," she said. "Did you open your window?" She glanced at the closed window, then back at Jamie. "Even your dog must be cold. I never saw Fireplug under the covers like that."

The mound beneath the blankets trembled, but Fireplug didn't come out.

"That dog is certainly acting strange," his mother continued. "I thought he liked the country."

"He got scared in the barn, Mom," Jamie explained.

"This is the man I told you about." He glanced at the chair by the wall. "He's gone!"

"Who's gone?"

"The man from the barn—Elmer. He was sitting there talking to me when you came in."

"Oh, come on, Jamie; don't pull any of your tricks on me tonight," Ellen warned. "Quit stalling and get into your pajamas. Fireplug, come out of there before you get too hot."

The room had warmed up again.

"Honest, Mom, that man was here," Jamie insisted. "I wonder where he went."

"That's enough, Jamie. The door I came in is the only one in your room, and nobody went out. If you're trying to make me believe there are ghosts in this house, then you're as silly as the neighbors who've been telling me all the scary things that happened here. Ghosts are all in your head. They're just things people use to scare children. Now go to bed. Get in there!"

Jamie scrambled into his pajamas and slid under the covers next to Fireplug. His mother bent over to kiss him, then tucked the covers around his shoulders.

"Good night, son," she said softly.

Jamie closed his eyes so she would think he was asleep. He heard the door close when she left.

CHAPTER FOUR

EASTER SUNDAY SCUFFLE

When Jamie was sure his mother had gone, he opened his eyes and pulled the cord on the lamp she had turned off. He looked around the room and leaned over the edge of the bed so he could see under it. No old man. He got out of bed and tiptoed over to the closet to look inside. Nothing but clothing.

"Elmer . . . you here?" he whispered.

There was no answer. Puzzled, he returned to the bed and pulled the covers off Fireplug. His dog came out, panting and wide-eyed.

"You scared of that old man?" Jamie asked. "He ain't gonna hurt you. Besides, he's gone."

Jamie settled himself into bed with Fireplug in his usual place atop the blankets. Where had Elmer gone? The old guy walked sort of slow and stiff, like he was hurting. He couldn't have moved fast enough to get past Jamie's mother without being seen.

Maybe there's a hidden passage in this room, Jamie thought. Maybe the money is stashed in it. He sat up to look at the high-ceilinged walls. But, if there was a secret hiding place and the money was in it, the old man would have taken it and ran. If he knew about it, that is.

Jamie decided he would search his room in the morning. He turned off the light and snuggled next to Fireplug. Old houses were supposed to have hidden closets and passageways and spooky halls that tramps used because they had nowhere else to go. Jamie's eyes closed.

In the morning his mother woke him when she came into the room. "Get up, Jamie. It's time to go to church."

She went to the closet and pulled out his Sunday suit. "I want you to look nice today," she said, glancing out the window. "I hope those clouds go away. Rain on Easter Sunday spoils everything."

Jamie sat up rubbing his eyes. "Gee, Mom, do I have to wear *that*?" Every time he had worn a suit in New York, the gang would tease him about it. He had to lick at least two of them to shut the rest up.

"Take Fireplug outside and then get yourself washed, young man. You'll be meeting your teacher for the first time today. Don't you want to make a good impression?"

Fireplug rose and stretched one hind leg, then the other.

"Come on, boy, let's go." Jamie got out of bed and walked toward the door.

"Put on your slippers," Ellen ordered.

"Aw, Mom, I'll be right back," Jamie replied, hurrying out with Fireplug at his heels.

Jamie frowned at the gaping hole in the screen before looking up at the grayish clouds floating in the sky. "You wait out here, boy, and don't go running off," he said to his pet.

When Jamie returned to his room, his mother was gone. The hated suit and a white shirt and underwear were neatly laid out on his bed. "Sissy stuff," he grumbled.

He brushed his teeth in the bathroom down the hall, and went back to his room to get dressed. No use arguing. When his mother told him to do something, she usually meant it. The only way to get around her was to do things she hadn't thought to forbid.

When Jamie and the other members of the family had gotten dressed, they walked out of the house and locked it up. Heading for the car, they took their usual places— Jim behind the wheel, Ellen in the front passenger seat, and Jamie and Margaret in the back. Jim started it up and they drove off to church, arriving at the same time as many other members of the congregation.

The people inside the church were divided roughly by age. Jamie's parents chatted briefly with a young woman who came to greet them, then left Margaret and Jamie with her while they joined the adults in another circle. Scooter was in his group, Jamie noticed, but then so was Margaret. He'd better behave or she would tattle, as usual.

"I'm Jan Carter," the teacher said with a friendly smile. She introduced Margaret and Jamie to the other children. When they were seated she began the lesson.

Jamie pretended to pay attention, but his mind was on other things. Where had the old man disappeared to last night? This morning after he dressed, .Jamie had hurriedly searched his room, feeling each crack and bump under the faded wallpaper and thumping around until his mother came in to ask what the banging was about.

Knowing that she thought he was lying about seeing Elmer the night before, Jamie just said he was inspecting his new quarters.

The old man had been sitting there talking to Jamie. That was no make-believe. He said he had been living on their farm, but he hadn't said why. Was he guarding the ten thousand dollars that was supposed to be hidden somewhere? No, he couldn't be, Jamie thought. If the old man had that much money he wouldn't be sleeping in barns and not eating. Jamie's stomach rumbled. The old guy must have been kidding when he said he never ate. Everybody had to eat.

Thinking about eating reminded Jamie of his dog. Fireplug was always hungry, or at least he pretended to be whenever Jamie ate. He would even eat bananas when Jamie ate them, and not many dogs did that.

The bottom of Jamie's foot began to itch, but he couldn't scratch it here. Jan Carter talked on about the Scriptures. Margaret sat primly with her hands folded in her lap like the other girls. Scooter stared at the teacher.

Jamie wished he could've stayed home with Fireplug. He had locked the little dog in his room to keep him out of trouble, and Fireplug didn't like to be shut in. Jamie brightened. Maybe old Fireplug would dig out the money if it was hidden in the room. Or find a secret passage, if there was one.

Then Jamie saw the group stirring. Some of them rose, and others felt under their chairs for personal belongings. Jamie knew the Sunday school lesson was over.

"Hi, Jamie," Scooter said. "Want to go hunt eggs?"

"Sure, Scooter, let's go."

"The little kids go first," Scooter explained. "They find

the easy ones. When we go out we're supposed to make
sure they have eggs in their baskets while we're getting
ours."

"You'll make sissies out of 'em," Jamie said. "In the
city every kid is on his own, no matter how little he is."
He stuck out his chest. "That's how me and Fireplug got
so tough. You bring your dog to church?"

"Can't. Ma makes me keep him in the kennel when
we go anywhere. Come on, Jamie, it's time we went out."

Jamie followed Scooter's lead, picking up an empty
basket from the pile outside the church. The clouds
overhead had grown thicker and people were staring upward while they talked about the coming rain and how
it could ruin the fun. Shouts of glee came when any of
the smaller children discovered a hidden nest of Easter
eggs. One little boy stood crying until an older girl took
his hand and put two colored eggs into his empty basket.

Scooter ran on ahead, but Jamie walked slowly along
until he found an egg. Disregarding the rules of the hunt,
he sat down on the grass to peel and eat it. He looked
up when Scooter returned.

"Needs salt," Jamie commented.

"You're not supposed to eat them yet," Scooter said.
"Aren't you going to look for more?"

"You said we had to fill the little kids' baskets first,
and I'm not about to work for them. Besides, Mom will
have baskets for me and Margaret when we get home."

"Well . . ." Scooter's voice trailed off. "I'd better help
or my Ma will be after me. See you later."

Jamie finished the egg and was brushing pieces of shell
from his trousers when another boy stopped in front of
him. Jamie's street-wise instincts were immediately

aroused and he sensed trouble.

"I'm Chuck Magruder," the boy said in a menacing tone.

Jamie sensed a dare and quickly sprang to his feet. "I'm Jim Boyd," he replied puffing himself up to assert his toughness.

"Jan said your name was *Jamie*," Chuck said mockingly. "You and your folks are squatting on our farm."

"*Your* farm? No way! My Dad bought it." Jamie replied.

"Pooh! My mother should've gotten the place when old Mathieson was killed. She's a cousin twice-removed of Lizzie Mathieson, and my Dad says it's rightfully hers."

"Well, it ain't!" Jamie planted his feet apart in imitation of the older boy. "You wanna try and take it?"

"Why, you little runt," Chuck sneered. "You think you can whip me?" His eyes gleamed. "Come on and try it, punk!"

Jamie sized up his opponent. Chuck was husky, almost fat in places, and about a head taller than Jamie. His brown hair was slicked in place over a round, beefy face. Like the other boys, he wore a suit, but the sleeves and legs were a little short. At the end of the shortened sleeves, Chuck's hands were knotted into fists while he waited Jamie's next move.

He didn't have to wait long. Without warning, Jamie lowered his head and butted the larger boy in the stomach. Chuck went backward with a grunt as the air swooshed out of him, landing on his back in the grass. In a flash, Jamie was on the other boy, punching as hard as he could.

Chuck's eyes bulged with surprise, but once he had gasped enough air to regain his wind, his fists came out swinging. He hit Jamie in the ribs and on the side of his face, as Jamie covered up and clung to his opponent like a bur.

Then Jamie was yanked up by the collar of his jacket. He looked at the scowling face of his father, and his heart sank. "Here we go again!" he said to himself.

"Get in the car, Jamie," his father growled.

"But, Dad . . ."

"Not another word! Get in the car right now!" The words were repeated with an iciness that sent a chill through Jamie.

When his father reached for Chuck's hand to help him to his feet, Jamie turned and walked slowly to the car. "Won't even let me explain," he grumbled to himself. His gaze averted the stares of the people watching him leave. "Pious old country hicks!" he muttered.

While Jamie sat by himself in the back seat of the car, Scooter came running to the window and grinned at him. "Mom says I can go home with you . . that is, if it's okay with you and your folks."

Jamie glanced up and Scooter shook his head. "Good gosh, Jamie, you're gonna have a shiner for sure! Why did you take on Chuck, of all people? He's whipped every boy in the county at least once."

"Aaah, he ain't so tough," Jamie retorted. "If my Dad hadn't pulled me away I would have whipped him."

Then Jamie's face brightened. "Hey, yeah, come on home with us. We'll hunt for that money," he said aloud to Scooter. "And Dad and Mom won't be so hard on me if you're around," he added to himself.

Ellen Boyd's face was grim when she and Margaret approached the car. Then she saw Scooter and smiled.

"Mom, this is Scooter Johnson," Jamie said quickly. "Yesterday I asked him to come home with me, and his Mom said he could."

"Well, that's fine, Jamie," she said, giving him a look before she got into the front seat that told him she would talk to him later about the fight.

"This is Margaret," Jamie told Scooter. "I guess you already met her in class."

Margaret sort of simpered in a way Jamie thought was disgusting, but Scooter grinned at her admiringly. "Hi again," he said, and Jamie nearly gagged. Margaret climbed over Jamie to sit by the other window and squeezed herself in so there was room for Scooter in the middle.

Jim Boyd opened the car door on the driver's side and looked into the back seat. He opened his mouth as if to say something, then closed it when he saw Scooter. He only nodded when Jamie introduced his friend, and gave Jamie the same kind of warning look his mother had. Jamie's mind began racing, planning ways to get Scooter to stay as long as possible. It was always handy to have company around when his parents were angry. However, this time his father was angry enough to dispense with his usual company manners.

"What was the fight about, Jamie?" he demanded.

"Chuck Magruder said we were squatting on his folks' farm. He called me a runt and a punk, and dared me to fight him. You don't want me to be a coward, do you, Dad?"

"I don't want you fighting all the time, either. Now, what's this about our property?"

Jamie repeated Chuck's words.

When he was finished, his parents traded apprehensive glances. There was an eerie silence of a few seconds before his father responded.

"So that was it!" he began. "I knew old Mathieson's will was contested in court, but it held. Well, Jamie, for your information and everyone else's, we do have a clear title to the farm. It's registered in the county clerk's office at the courthouse, and anyone who's interested can see it. You disgraced yourself by fighting at church, but now that I know what it was about, we'll overlook it this time."

He started the car and put it in gear. "Let's get home and eat," he went on. "I hope everyone is good and hungry. I saw a ham as big as a whole pig being cooked early this morning."

"And flies coming in the hole in the screen because of the good smell," Margaret said, glancing smugly at Jamie.

Jamie returned her glance with an angry one of his own, but she only made a face at him.

"You'd better fix the door right after dinner, Jamie," his father said. "The flies are worse because of the coming rain. I'm sure your guest will understand."

"Sure. I'll help him, Mr. Boyd." Scooter said. "We were only going to hunt for the money, and it's probably hidden so well we'll never find it."

"From what Sheriff Griffith told me, I imagine the farm has already been searched from one end to the other," Jamie's father said.

"If there's a hidden passage in our house, the money could still be in it," Jamie said in a voice that was hopeful. "Maybe people didn't get into the house after the Mathiesons died. Maybe it was locked up."

"Not many empty houses are locked in the country," Scooter said. "People just break in when nobody's around."

"Well, it would sure be nice to find a hidden treasure," Jamie insisted. "Wouldn't it be nice to find a lot of money, Dad?"

"It sure would, son."

"How silly!" Jamie's mother said, turning to look at them. "I suppose the story of how Mr. Mathieson died is true, but the rest of it, complete with 'ghosts', was made up by people with nothing else to do. Nobody would be foolish enough to bury ten thousand dollars if they had it, and there are no such things as ghosts. You know that, don't you, Scooter?"

"Yes, ma'am," Scooter answered, but there was a look of doubt on his face.

The clouds had thickened while they talked, and now a streak of lightning flashed across the dark sky. Thunder rumbled in the distance. Jamie grinned. A stormy day would be perfect for exploring the attic with Scooter and having some fun.

CHAPTER FIVE

EXPLORING THE ATTIC

By the time Jamie's stomach was comfortably stuffed with Easter dinner, the storm had arrived. Lightning flashed and thunder shook the old house. He felt Fireplug trembling against his leg. His dog was under the table within reach of the tidbits Jamie fed him throughout the meal.

"I hate storms," Margaret said. "I don't see why we couldn't have moved to California where the sun shines all the time."

Her mother laughed. "That's another myth. California has rain and storms and even earthquakes at times that are much more frightening than thunder and lightning."

"Why don't you let her go there if she wants to?" Jamie taunted.

"Jamie, please? Let's not start an argument," his mother said. "Why don't you and Scooter find something to do?" She glanced out the window. "It's raining too hard

to go outside, but I can unpack some of the games we brought with us."

Jamie groaned, and his father gave him a sympathetic look. "Maybe the boys can make it to the barn, Ellen. When I was a kid we thought it was fun to climb up to the hayloft and play."

"They'll get wet going out there, Jim," she said.

"Then can we explore the top floors of the house?" Jamie asked in a voice betraying his eagerness. "Maybe Scooter and me can find the money old Mathieson hid."

"There's no . ." his mother began, then stopped after a wink from her husband said it was okay.

"Why not?" Jim asked. "Hunting treasure on a rainy day should be fun. And while you're up there, you might want to clean up the cobwebs and dirt. Take some dust mops along, and stack up the junk that's lying around. Your mother will get whatever you need to clean things up."

"Thanks, Dad." Jamie rose, and then paused. "Oh, do you want me to fix the screen first?"

"No, son, you go ahead and start on the attic. I'll put a new piece of screen in the door."

Armed with a broom and dust mop, Jamie and Scooter raced up the stairs to the second floor with Fireplug at their heels. The steps to the third floor were enclosed in a hallway with a door separating them from the lower part of the house. Jamie paused at the closed door.

"Dad thinks he's putting one over on us, getting us to clean the attic for him." He laughed. "But I got out of fixing that darned old screen door, didn't I?"

Scooter nodded. "My folks do the same thing. They use psy . . . psy . . . heck, I can't hardly say it." He swallowed and tried again. "Psy*chology*! That's it!" he exclaimed. Then a grin crinkled his eyes. "Beats a whippin', don't it?"

"Yeah," Jamie agreed.

He opened the door and looked upward into the gloominess there. "Lots of spider webs," he said, glancing over his shoulder at Scooter. "You 'fraid of spiders?"

"Naw," Scooter replied bravely. "Want me to go ahead and swing the broom at 'em?"

"Just get the ones I miss." Jamie started up the steps with the mop in front of him, swishing away at the thick curtain of webs and dust. Fireplug zipped eagerly through Jamie's spread legs and sat down at the top to wait, dusty and triumphant.

The third floor had a series of rooms on either side of a narrow hall. After opening several doors and finding nothing but bare walls and more cobwebs, Jamie shook his head. "We can check these later for secret panels and stuff. Let's go to the attic and see what's there."

He walked along the hall staring up at the ceiling until he saw the square outline of a trap door. A rickety ladder hung from two rusty iron hooks in the wall. Jamie staggered under its weight as he pulled it down and carried it to a spot below the door. Scooter rushed to help him, and with much grunting and straining, the boys got the ladder in position against the panel in the ceiling. They pushed until the trap door was raised.

"It's kind of shaky," Scooter said apprehensively.

"Aaah, it'll hold us," Jamie replied confidently.

Jamie took the lead in climbing the rungs. At the top of the ladder he hunched his shoulders against the wood and heaved as hard as he could. The door fell backward with a crash against the attic floor. A thick cloud of dust arose, flying up into his eyes before he could close them, and he sneezed as some of it also drifted into his nose.

The temperature was noticeably colder in the attic. Jamie climbed in first, rubbing his eyes and nose to clear out the dust. As Scooter followed Jamie through the opening, the two of them shivered and their teeth began chattering. Jamie raised his shirt collar and drew it up around his neck to keep out the chill.

After a quick look around, Jamie peered through the opening at Fireplug down below. The little dog had his front feet on the first rung.

"Stay there, boy," he told the dog. He glanced at Scooter and added, "Sit!"

"Must be getting colder outside," Scooter said. " 'Long about Easter the rains usually warm up, but this one feels like it's coming down from the Arctic."

Jamie turned from the trap door to squint into the shadowy attic. Now and then streaks of lightning lit up the space and threw weird shadows against the rafters and beams. Gables divided the attic into little rooms. Old iron cots, many with legs rusted in a heap below them, were all around. Boxes and cartons spilled rags and junk into dusty piles.

"It sure is spooky up here," Scooter said.

Suddenly a strange sound startled him. "Whoo-oo-oo . . . whoo-oo-oo."

Scooter jumped. "What was that?"

"What was what?" Jamie asked. When Scooter looked the other way, Jamie made the sound again. "Whoo-oo-oo . . whoo-oo-oo."

Scooter spun around. "There it is again! You heard

that, I know!"

"Heard what?" Jamie's eyes were round and innocent.

"Something went 'whoo-oo-oo, whoo-oo-oo'."

"Maybe there's a ghost up here," Jamie commented innocently. "I should have brought a flashlight. It's hard to see. Let's start looking through this junk and see what's in it."

"I want to know what made that noise," Scooter insisted. "I think I'll go ask your father for a light."

"You scared?"

Scooter's face grew stubborn. "No, I'm not *scared*," he said. "I just want to be able to see what I'm doing."

"Well, go ahead then. I'll start while you're getting it." Jamie picked up a rag that had once been a shirt.

When Scooter disappeared down the opening, Jamie grinned. Good thing he didn't believe in ghosts himself. His own hooting was so spooky it had given him goose bumps.

"That wasn't a very nice thing to do," a voice behind him said.

Jamie whirled and saw Elmer sitting on a big box. "How did you get up *here*?" he demanded.

Elmer sighed. "I thought you would have guessed by now. I'm a ghost, Jamie." The old man frowned. "Only I don't go around hooting like an owl. I have some chains I can rattle, but they're so darned heavy I don't bother carrying them around much any more."

The startled look left Jamie's face, and he doubled up laughing. When he could finally control himself, he looked at Elmer. "No kidding?"

The gray head nodded. "How come you aren't scared?"

"Mom told me there are no such things as ghosts when

I was still a little kid. You want to go tell *her* you're a ghost?"

The air in the attic grew even colder as Elmer sighed again. "Most kids run like crazy when I show up out of nowhere." His voice was sad. "You don't believe in much of anything you can't spend, do you?"

"You might be wacko, but you're no ghost," Jamie said. "People just make up ghosts to scare little kids."

He heard Scooter climbing the ladder and turned to watch him come up carrying a flashlight. The beam it put out illuminated the path in front of him. Behind him Fireplug crawled through the opening and flopped, panting, in a cloud of dust.

"Hey, Fireplug's learned to climb a ladder!" Jamie said, patting the dust off him. "Bring the light over here, Scooter."

Scooter swung the light on Jamie and hopscotched his way around the junk to where Jamie stood. Fireplug rose, then stood with one front paw lifted as though he were frozen.

"This is Elmer," Jamie said. He turned to the box where the old man had been sitting, but he wasn't there.

A clap of thunder crashed against the roof and Jamie flinched. Fireplug's ears shot up and he dove through the trap door. A thump and a howl of pain accompanied his landing on the floor below.

"What did you say?" Scooter asked when the noise died down.

"That old man was up here, but now he's gone." Jamie walked over to where Elmer had been sitting and looked behind the box.

A groan sounded softly in his ear. "Get off my bunions!" a pained voice whispered.

Jamie panicked and jumped back, looking all around him. The hair on the nape of his neck prickled.

"I heard another noise, didn't you?" Scooter asked, shining the light into the darkest shadows. "Where'd the old man go?"

Jamie was puzzled. Where *had* Elmer gone this time? The walls and ceiling were open, showing the underside of the wood siding that covered the house. There couldn't be a secret door or panel there. He shivered. Gosh, it was cold!

"Something funny's going on here," Jamie said. "That old man said he was a *ghost!* Can you beat that?"

Another crash of thunder shook the roof. The room glowed weirdly from a flash of lightning. Jamie glanced at Scooter. "What's wrong with you?"

Scooter swallowed, his eyes wide with fright. "If he can come and go like you say, maybe he is a ghost. Maybe old Mathieson still haunts the place, like folks say." His voice broke on the last word and came out as a squeak when he added, "Let's get out of here!"

"Go ahead and run like a rabbit if you're afraid," Jamie said. "I'm going to find out what's going on. I bet there's another trap door somewhere around here, or else he's hiding in one of these crates."

Jamie stooped to push some of the junk aside while he examined the floor, then moved over a few steps and repeated his actions. Scooter kept the light on Jamie, although it quivered in his shaking hand.

Jamie glanced up. "It's just the storm making you so jumpy. You heard Mom say there were no ghosts, didn't you?"

The air in the attic warmed. Jamie folded his collar back
down. He looked toward the trap door when Fireplug's
shaggy head came through, followed by the rest of him
as he crawled over the edge into the room.

"Come here, boy," Jamie called.

Fireplug paused a moment before his short legs churned
up dust as he raced across the floor, hurling himself into
Jamie's arms.

"What's wrong with you, Fireplug? You're acting like
a goofball," Jamie muttered.

Fireplug whined and licked Jamie's face.

"Even your dog is scared," Scooter said. "Let's go
downstairs."

"Aaah, storms scare Fireplug, that's all. And that's the
only thing he's scared of," Jamie replied. He put the little dog on the floor. "Help me find another trap door,
boy."

With Fireplug beside him Jamie continued to push
boxes aside and move piles of junk into the center of the
big room. His feet made hollow sounds on the wooden
floor. Some of the planks squeaked when his weight bore
down on them. Clouds of dust rose, then settled back.
Even the rusty old cots were shoved this way and that as
Jamie examined the floor.

"Wonder what all these beds were for," Scooter said.
"There was a big farm sale out here after the Mathiesons
died, and all their furniture was s'posed to be sold. I guess
no one thought to look up here."

"They're too rotten to be worth much," Jamie
commented.

Scooter watched as Jamie continued moving things
around, flashing the light back and forth through the

attic. Then he walked over and helped Jamie pile the junk into a neat stack.

Suddenly Fireplug barked. He scratched madly at the big brick chimney at the back of the attic. Jamie walked over to feel the rough bricks.

"Hey, Scooter, come here!" Jamie called excitedly. He had found a black iron ring fastened in the bricks. He tried to pull it out, but it refused to move.

Scooter came running, shining the light over Jamie's shoulder.

"Help me pull this thing," Jamie said.

Scooter wrapped his arms around Jamie's waist and pulled backward. With a dry, rasping noise, the ring came loose in a square of bricks that left a gaping hole in the chimney wall. Jamie went down, still holding the heavy brick panel, and landed on top of Scooter. Fireplug charged toward the chimney, barking with excitement as he tried to reach the opening.

"There's your other door," Jamie hollered over Fireplug's barking. "That's where the old man went out!"

CHAPTER SIX

THE SECRET PASSAGE

Jamie freed himself from Scooter's legs and rolled over onto the brick panel. Then he got up, leaving the panel on the floor, and went to look into the black opening. Fireplug backed away and sat down, panting from his exertions.

"See?" Jamie said. "I told you there was another door where the old man could get out. Some ghost!"

Scooter came up beside Jamie. He stuck his head into the opening and looked down, thrusting the flashlight as far down as he could, trying to see through the sooty curtain below.

"Oh, yeah?" he said. "Then how come the cobwebs aren't broken? Nobody's been in here for a long time, I bet!"

Jamie tried to ignore the fear that was growing inside him. "Where does it go?" he wondered aloud. "If we had a rope, I could get down there and see."

"It's awfully dirty down there," Scooter said slowly. "Look, let's go tell your father about this and see what he says."

Jamie thought for a moment and nodded in agreement. "I guess he's got the screen fixed by now." He looked around the attic. "Doesn't seem to be anything but junk up here. Besides, we need a rope. Okay, let's go ask Dad to come up."

Jamie picked up Fireplug and climbed through the trap door. He went down the ladder followed by Scooter.

When the boys reached the living room, Jamie's mother looked up in surprise. "For goodness' sake! How did you get so dirty, Jamie? Scooter is still clean."

"I worked harder than he did, Mom," he replied. Then, addressing his father, he said, "Dad, we found a secret passage we want you to help us check out."

"Oh?" Jamie's father said, laying down the newspaper he was reading. "Where is it? Lead the way, boys," he added, rising from his chair.

"We'd better take a rope along," Jamie said. He glanced at his mother. "I'll change my clothes as I go by my room."

"It's a little late for that. Anyway, your clothes will wash," she said with a sigh.

"Why do we need a rope, son?" Jim asked.

"So you can lower me into the passage, Dad."

"Now wait just one minute," Jim said. "Before we get a rope or you change your clothes or anything, suppose I take a look at this—whatever it is you think you found."

Jamie shifted impatiently from one foot to the other. "Okay, Dad, but let's get going. You don't want somebody else to get the money, do you?"

"There's no . . ." Jamie's mother began, but she broke it off, shaking her head and clamping her lips shut.

"If the money is there, Jamie, I doubt it will leave in the next few minutes," Jim said. "But come on . . . let's see what we can find."

The boys raced up the stairs. Jamie's father followed at a slower pace. Fireplug ran up and down the steps as though to hurry him along.

In the attic Jamie took his father's hand and pulled him over to the chimney. "There, Dad, see? There was like a door in the hole with a ring to yank it out."

Jim stuck his head into the opening, then withdrew it, brushing a web from his hair. "That might be just a hole to make cleaning the chimney easier, Jamie. Old houses like this used to be heated by stoves, but the flues in the wall were plugged up when electric heating was installed."

"Aw, it *has* to be a secret passage, Dad." Jamie insisted. He stuck his head into the hole and looked up, letting out a shout that echoed on the old bricks.

"Hey, look up here!" He reached up and pulled a dirty coil of rope from a hook above the opening. The rope was rotten, but its shape was still plain to see: it was a ladder.

"See, Dad?" he said, presenting it triumphantly to Jim.

His father took the rope and carefully examined it. "You're right, Jamie. This must have been an escape hatch of some kind." He looked around the attic at the rusty old iron cots. "This house is over a hundred years old. Maybe this was one of the hideouts used by runaway slaves before the Civil War."

"My Pa told me the slaves used to go up through here on their way to Canada," Scooter said. "I bet they hid in this attic until it was safe for them to leave."

"A station on the 'Underground Railroad'," Jim mused, remembering his American history from school days. "This old house must have *some* stories to tell."

"Hot dog!" Jamie said eagerly. "Now do you believe me, Dad? Get a rope and lower me down so I can see where it goes."

"Don't be silly, son. If this is an outlet, there's got to be an outside exit somewhere on the property. It would be easier to hunt for it and go in that way than to get all dirty in the chimney."

"Well, let's go then!" Jamie said, snapping his fingers. "Come on, Fireplug, you can sniff it out for me."

"Now wait a minute, Jamie," his father said. "It's still raining and your mother doesn't want you running around outside. Besides, I think you've done enough exploring for one day. Get your raincoat on and we'll take Scooter home before his folks begin to worry about him."

"Aaah .." Jamie grumbled in protest, but his father's face held firm. There wasn't even any sun to prolong the daylight, and by the time they returned from taking Scooter home, it would again be time to collect the dumb old eggs.

The rain stopped before they dropped Scooter off at his house. The clouds parted to let the rays of the setting sun sparkle on the water clinging to the spring foliage. The countryside smelled damp and fresh and newly born. A colt kicked up his heels in a pasture they passed, then lowered his head to the bright green grass.

It was twilight when Jamie picked up the egg basket and headed for the barn. Fireplug bounced along beside him, detouring to splash through puddles. Jamie stopped and hesitated at the door of the barn. Fireplug stuck his neck out as far as he could to sniff inside. Feelings of doubt began to gnaw at Jamie's insides. Would Elmer suddenly show up again? He sure was a spooky old geezer. Could he really be a ghost? Naah! How could Elmer be a ghost when Jamie's mother was so sure there weren't any such things? Most likely he was just some old tramp playing games with him.

Jamie mustered up his courage and marched inside the barn. With an air of confidence, he began to collect the eggs. The setting hen was in one of the nests, but now he knew how to handle the old biddy. He simply lifted her out with both hands and picked up her eggs before she could return.

Fireplug moved around warily at first, but then grew bolder, poking his nose into corners and under the roosts. He stopped suddenly near the grain bin, sniffed the dirt beneath the old floor, then began feverishly digging there.

"Get 'em, boy," Jamie said. He grinned at the shower of dirt flying from Fireplug's busy paws.

By the time the last egg was in the basket, all that could be seen of Fireplug was his small rear end with hind legs firmly set, and showers of dirt coming out between them. Jamie set the basket down by the door and went to see what his dog was doing.

"Whatcha got there, Fireplug?"

The stubby tail wagged, but the digging continued.

There was a yelp, and Fireplug backed out from beneath the grain bin with a huge bone in his mouth. He laid it at Jamie's feet, and quickly returned to his hole. Seconds later, he brought out something else: a big dog collar. Jamie looked at it closely, excitement beginning to build up inside him. The Mathieson's missing dog! Had he gotten stuck under the grain bin?

Jamie knelt beside Fireplug and scooped dirt out of the way. The smell under the old bin was musty and dank. Jamie wrinkled his nose at the pungent rotting odor of decomposed wood and dirt, but he kept working until he reached a nest-like space. It was too dark to see inside, but after Fireplug dragged another bone out, Jamie reached in to feel around. His hand touched metal and closed on the object. Feeling it sink into his finger, he quickly pulled it out and saw it was a knife. He dropped it and thrust the cut finger into his mouth.

"Pfft," he sputtered, removing the finger from his mouth and spitting out dirt and blood. He wrapped his handkerchief around the wound, still flicking his tongue in and out to expel the remaining dirt from his mouth.

The knife was big and rusty. It was a hunting blade that was supposed to fold into its bone handle, but it had rusted into the open position. It would take a good soaking in oil to clean it. Gathering up the dog collar and knife from the floor, Jamie turned to go.

Fireplug came out of the hole with a doughnut-shaped metal object clamped in his teeth and laid it at Jamie's feet. Jamie picked it up and brushed the dirt from it. It was an iron ring like the one in the chimney trap door. With a shrug, Jamie returned the ring to Fireplug and he carried it in his mouth while he trotted to the door. Jamie carefully placed the knife and the collar in the basket with the eggs and headed for the house.

His mother turned from the stove when they entered the kitchen. "Wipe your feet, Jamie," she said, followed quickly by an "Oh, no!" as she saw the trail of muddy paw prints leading under the table.

"I'll get 'em, Mom," Jamie said. He laid the knife on the sink and grabbed a handful of paper towels to remove the tracks. Then he went under the table and wiped the rest of the mud off Fireplug's paws. When he came out, his mother was examining the knife.

"Where did you find this old thing, Jamie?" she asked, noticing for the first time his handkerchief-wrapped finger. "Did you cut yourself?"

"Just a little bit, Mom. It's nothin', really."

She removed the dirty handkerchief and held his finger under the tap to let the water clean it. "Good thing you just had a tetanus shot." She handed him a towel. "I'll put some peroxide on it."

"What's going on?" Jim asked as he entered.

"Jamie cut his hand on that old knife. I'll be right back," Ellen replied.

"Look, Dad, I think Fireplug found what's left of Mathieson's missing dog. This knife was buried with the bones. You suppose the dog was stabbed to death?" Jamie took the collar from the basket of eggs and laid it down on the counter next to the knife.

Jamie's father held the knife under the running water and removed as much of the dirt as he could. He tried to close it, but the slot for the blade was still clogged.

"It sure is an old knife," he said, squinting. "Hand-carved, too. I'll take this in to the sheriff tomorrow, Jamie. He might be able to use it as evidence."

"You think whoever stabbed Mr. Mathieson killed his dog, too?" Jamie asked.

"I don't know, son. We'd better let the sheriff figure it out."

"Well, look, Dad. If someone killed that dog with a knife, it had to be someone the dog knew."

"Why do you say that, Jamie?"

"Because a stranger couldn't get close enough . . . especially if the dog was a good watchdog like the sheriff said."

His father nodded. "That's right." He smiled at Jamie. "You're a pretty good detective. Now if you find the hidden money, we'll be able to pay off the mortgage on this place," he added jokingly.

"You wanna go hunt for the other end of the secret passage tonight, Dad?"

"No, he doesn't," his mother answered as she entered. "And neither do you, Jamie. It's too late to go out digging around." She swabbed the cut on his finger with a cotton ball dipped in hydrogen peroxide and covered it with a Band-Aid.

"She's right, Jamie," his father agreed. "We'll take a look when you get home from school tomorrow. I want you to sack in early tonight. The school bus will be here at seven, so you'll have to get up early. Now, let's eat our supper before it gets cold."

"That's a good idea," his mother said. "Margaret, did you wash your hands?"

"I haven't been grubbing in the dirt, Mom." Margaret said, bringing a dish of potatoes to the table and taking her seat.

Jamie slumped into a chair. Why did grown-ups always put a damper on fun? He wanted to go look for the other end of the secret passage *now*, and not have to wait through a whole day of school. Besides, the exit must be well hidden or somebody would have found it before now.

Why not just drop down the chimney from the attic and find out where it went? That would be the fast way.

When he put down his fork, his mother ordered him to bed, even though it was only eight o'clock. "You, too, Margaret," she added.

"Okay, Mom," Jamie said. "But, you don't need to come tuck me in any more. I ain't no little kid."

"Don't say 'ain't,'" she said. "I know you're growing up, but I'm not. I still like to be kissed good night, so I don't think I'll stop just yet."

Jamie grinned at his mother. He had to admire the way she always turned the tables on him somehow, even if he didn't get his own way. Women were so smoochy. Dad had agreed with him on a handshake when Jamie told him he was too big for kissing; why couldn't Mom? Men were more reasonable than women.

He turned and hurried to his room. Maybe if he went to bed quickly, so would his parents, and then he could sneak up to the attic and explore the chimney. "Wish I knew where to find a rope," he muttered. "Hey, Fireplug, find me a rope."

Fireplug cocked his shaggy head at Jamie's words, but he just sat down.

When his mother came in, Jamie was under the covers in his pajamas.

"It's warmer in here now than it was last night," she said. "I think the storm has passed, so tomorrow should be nice." Then, letting out a sigh, she added, "Your eye looks terrible, Jamie. I wish you wouldn't fight with your playmates."

"Playmates!" he scoffed. "Mom, I'm almost a man, but you keep treating me like I'm a little kid."

"Well, you're *my* little kid," she said. "And you'll still be my kid when you're a father yourself and forty years old." Her smile was tender. "Mothers are like that, Jamie. Now, do I get an Easter kiss?"

Jamie sat up. "Sure, Mom." He puckered his lips and raised his face to hers, smacking loudly when their mouths touched. "Okay?"

"Okay," she replied as she arose. "I'll get a piece of steak for that eye. Maybe if you keep it on all night, it won't be so . . so discolored in the morning."

When she had gone, Jamie flopped back against the pillow in disgust. She'd be back fussing over his eye and he'd have to wait even longer before he could go up to the attic. He yawned and stretched. "Maybe I'll just take a little nap first," he thought. His eyes closed.

CHAPTER SEVEN

"A TOUGH KID LIKE YOU"

When Jamie awoke he had trouble opening his eyes. A weight pressed on one of them and both were bandaged with a soft cloth. He groped for the knot on the cloth and untied it. A limp piece of meat fell on the bed. Fireplug sniffed it, then picked it up.

"Put that down, boy," he commanded. "Raw meat's bad for you. It'll give you worms." Jamie took the meat and wrapped it in the cloth.

His mother stuck her head around the edge of the door. "You awake? Time to get ready for school, Jamie. I'll have breakfast on the table by the time you're dressed."

"All right, Mom." Jamie looked at the light coming in the window. He had slept the night away and now the secret passage would have to wait.

In the bathroom, he stared at himself in the mirror. Wow! His eye was all different colors. The raw meat hadn't done much good.

71

By the time the school bus honked for them, Jamie and
Margaret were ready and waiting. Fireplug flopped out
on the veranda as though he knew he would have to wait
all day while Jamie was at school.

"Mornin'," the driver said. "I'm Dan Carter. My
daughter Jan said she met you two in church. I'll be driving you to school."

Margaret said good morning and then walked back to
take a seat beside one of the girls she had met in Sunday
school. Jamie nodded. There was only one empty seat
left—the one next to Chuck Magruder.

Jamie planted his feet apart in the aisle and glared at
the other boy.

Chuck glared back, then sneered. "You're carrying my
trademark, kid, so you might as well sit down." When
Jamie had seated himself, Chuck continued. "You got off
lucky 'cause your old man grabbed you."

"*You* got off lucky 'cause my old man grabbed me,"
Jamie answered defiantly. "You wouldn't last long where
I come from."

"Oh, yeah? You're a tough one, eh? Wait til you meet
old Mathieson's ghost. You'll scream for your mamma!"

"Only a dumbbell like you . ." Jamie began, and then
stopped when an idea came to him. "Oh, you must mean
the old man who shows up every once in a while. I've
already met him. He showed me the secret passage where
old Mathieson hid his money."

"Huh?" Chuck's mouth dropped open.

Jamie nodded. "Yeah. And all I have to do is go get
it when I have time."

"You're lying!" Chuck said. "Pa and me searched every
inch of that farm."

"You didn't have a *ghost* to tell you where it was."
Jamie looked around the bus and lifted a hand to
Scooter sitting back near Margaret.

"Where?" Chuck demanded, grabbing Jamie's arm.
"Where'd you find a secret passage?" He roughly pulled
Jamie toward him.

Jamie jerked his arm away. "Let go! Don't make me
belt you again!"

Before Chuck could react, the bus stopped in front of
the school and Jamie got up. Old Chuck would have
something to think about today. He grinned as Scooter
met him in the aisle. "Want to get the money today after
school?" Jamie asked in a loud voice.

"What?" Scooter replied.

"The old ghost said he'd meet me when I get home,"
Jamie added.

Scooter grabbed Jamie's arm and hurried him out the
door. "Hey, you shouldn't talk that way where Chuck can
hear you. He's told everybody the money belongs to his
father . . if there is any money."

"Aaah, he's a loudmouth!" Jamie scoffed. "You should
have seen him when I told him I'd met old Mathieson's
ghost." Jamie laughed.

"Well, don't let him corner you, Jamie. He'll beat you
up if you don't tell him what he wants to know."

"Let him try!"

Inside the school, Jamie had to report to the main office and sign enrollment papers. Margaret did, too, and
then they went their separate ways. Jamie liked school,
but he wouldn't dare admit it. Back in New York the gang
thought anyone who got good grades was a sissy, so he
goofed off whenever he could, spending a lot of time sit-

ting in the principal's office. That had been a real drag.

Class followed class, and Jamie was given assignments in the various books he received for each of them. He wondered how the rest of the boys felt about school. They behaved better than the guys in New York, at least in his class. Scooter was a grade higher, and Chuck was beyond him. Jamie would have to check with Scooter on the way home and feel his way around until he got the scoop on how to act.

By the time school was over, Jamie had an armful of books and a lot of homework. Scooter had saved him a seat on the bus, and Jamie slid in, flopping the books on the seat between them.

"Look at all this homework," he grumbled. "Do you do yours?"

"Sure, why not?" Scooter replied. "I don't want to be a dummy. If Pa can swing the tuition, I'm gonna go to college and be an engineer. They make more money than farmers."

Jamie grunted. "You coming over tonight?"

"Pa said I'd better leave treasure hunting for the weekends. I have chores and homework to do. By the time I get through with them and eat supper, it'll be bedtime."

Jamie grabbed his books when the bus pulled to a stop in front of his house. "See you tomorrow, Scooter."

Margaret reached the open door ahead of him. When she stepped to the ground, Fireplug darted around her to jump on Jamie.

"Come on, boy, I'll race you to the house," Jamie said, and ran ahead of his sister to the kitchen.

His mother had baked a cake. Jamie's eyes lit up when he saw the big slab she had cut for him. There was a smaller piece for Margaret and two glasses of milk.

"That sure looks good, Mom," Jamie commented in a voice betraying his eagerness. "Soon as I finish it, I want to hunt for the other end of the secret passage. Is Dad here?"

"He hasn't returned from town yet, Jamie," she replied. "You'd better wait for the weekend to do your exploring. By the time you get your homework and chores done, it'll be time for supper and too dark."

"Aw, gee . . ." Jamie sighed. Did all parents gang up on their kids and say the same thing, he wondered.

"When you finish your cake, change your clothes and do your homework . . . or collect the eggs first, if you'd rather. You too, Margaret."

"Is she s'posed to collect the eggs?" Jamie asked hopefully.

"No, I'm not," Margaret answered in her usual smug tone. "I'll be helping Mom with dinner when I've done my homework, so don't think you can push your work onto me."

"Stop arguing, children," Ellen said.

Jamie slipped the last piece of cake to Fireplug before gathering up his books and racing up to his room. He threw the books on the bed and gave a start as a sharp, "Ouch!" pierced the air.

Fireplug yelped and whirled toward the door, but it was closed. He dove under the bed as fast as he could.

Elmer appeared, his long, aging frame stretched out on Jamie's bed. "Watch where you're throwing things," he said gruffly. "Books have sharp corners."

"Holy smoke!" Jamie exclaimed.

"I ain't holy and I ain't smoke," Elmer said. "I'm a

ghost."

The room was icy, and Jamie shivered. "What're you doing on my bed?"

"I was sleeping until you threw your books at me."

"I didn't know you were there," Jamie replied slowly, regaining his composure. "Why did you disappear when Scooter came by yesterday?"

"One boy's enough trouble." Elmer's voice was tired. "I thought you were smart enough to figure out who killed old Mathieson if I helped a little, so why should I bother to show myself for anybody else? It takes a lot of energy to make myself appear, you know."

"Are you old Mathieson's ghost?" Jamie asked

Elmer sat up. "No, I'm not, but I have to hang around here until his murderer is caught. I'm one of St. Peter's private investigators . . a P.I." He sighed. "Only, I'm not getting any younger. This is my last case and I can't wait to retire. Nobody was around until you and your family showed up, so I've been waiting."

"But other people came out to look for the money," Jamie said. "Why didn't you get one of them to help you?"

"Every time I tried they'd scream and run," Elmer replied, shaking his head. "Nobody will admit flat out they believe in ghosts, but they sure take off fast when one appears." He grinned. "I knew a tough kid like you wouldn't be afraid."

"That's 'cause I don't believe you're a ghost," Jamie said stubbornly.

"Well, believe what you want." Elmer replied, a trace of annoyance evident in his voice. "You found the knife that killed the Mathieson dog, and that's a good clue. If Sheriff Griffith uses his head, he'll come out and maybe figure out who killed the old man."

"Do you know who did it?" Jamie asked.

"No, I don't," Elmer answered. "I wasn't sent here until after the crime was committed, and I can't go home til it's solved. Meanwhile, my arthritis is getting worse from hanging around this old house, and that barn and attic . . ." His voice trailed off.

"Well, Mom says I have to do homework and gather the dumb old eggs, and by that time it'll be dark." Jamie said. Suddenly, a thought came to him. "Hey look, I'll make a deal with you. If you lower me down the chimney on a rope, maybe *I* can solve the mystery and you can retire. And maybe we'll find the money, too. Will you?"

"No," was Elmer's abrupt reply. "When I was a boy I cut classes and didn't do homework and I grew up to be a bum. You don't want that, do you? If I had gone to college, I'd be a commissioner now instead of just a private eye. You do as your mother says. I can wait until the weekend. And, if you don't mind, I'll use your bed until you're ready for it."

"You aren't much help," Jamie grumbled. "If you're s'posed to solve this case, why don't we get going?"

"We will . . . this weekend. I'll be all rested up by then."

Jamie scowled as he began changing his clothes. It was bad enough having two parents on your back without having an old guy who could show up any time he wanted to give you orders. Was he really a ghost like he said? Magicians could make things appear and disappear. Maybe that's what he was.

When Jamie returned to the bed, he opened one of the books. "You gonna help me with this?" he asked Elmer.

Elmer turned his back to Jamie. "I told you . . . I'm

a dummy when it comes to school. I didn't get past the fourth grade. I'm going to sleep so I can help you on Saturday." A small snore followed.

With a sigh, Jamie began his homework. Two hours later he closed the last book. "Hey, Elmer, you gonna help me gather eggs?"

Another snore answered him, and Jamie got up. At the door, he paused. "Come on, Fireplug."

A shaggy head poked out from beneath the bed. Seeing the open door, Fireplug shot toward it and raced into the hall. Jamie slammed the door behind him.

The hens were all on the roosts, and Jamie gathered the eggs in record time. Fireplug went to dig under the grain bin, but Jamie called him away.

"Leave those bones alone, boy. We'll have a funeral for that old hound Saturday. A good dog shouldn't be scattered around like that." He trudged back toward the house. "That is, if I ever get time to do anything but homework and chores," he muttered.

"Find any more clues?" his father asked when Jamie reached the kitchen. "Sheriff Griffith said that knife is the first lead he's gotten. He said you'd be a real deputy if you keep going like you've been."

"Whose knife was it, Dad?"

"That's what the sheriff is going to try and find out, Jamie."

"Did you tell him about the dog collar and bones?"

His father nodded. "Yes. He said if he can find out who killed the Mathiesons' watchdog, it might lead him to who killed Mr. Mathieson. He's going to examine the evidence and then he wants to come out here and investigate."

Jamie sat down. "Dad, do you think there might be

such a thing as ghosts? Mom says not."

"Well . . I kind of doubt there are. Why do you ask, son?"

"That old man keeps showing up, and he told me he's a ghost," Jamie replied.

"Now, Jamie, don't start on that again," his mother said as she carried steaming dishes to the table.

"But, Mom, he was up in my room this afternoon . . . sleeping on my bed," Jamie insisted. "Didn't you see him go up?"

"Ghosts wouldn't tell you that they're ghosts," Jim said.

"Well, what *do* ghosts do?" Jamie asked.

"There are no ghosts, Jamie," his mother said. "Haven't I always told you that? Your imagination is running away with you. An old house creaks and the wind whistles through the cracks. You imagined this old man and now you think he's really there."

"He said he was going to use my bed until I needed it, Mom. Will you go see if he's still there? Sneak in so he won't hear you."

"I'll go up," Jim said. "If some old tramp is prowling around the house, Sheriff Griffith might have more work to do."

Jamie watched his father leave the room. Elmer was a nice old guy, and he sure didn't want him busted just for coming into their house. Maybe he shouldn't have told on him.

When his father returned, he was frowning. "There's nobody in your room Jamie. It's nice and warm and ready for you to turn in, if you're done with your homework."

"The old man must've left, Dad," Jamie insisted. "Every time he shows up, it gets cold. Doesn't that prove he's a ghost?"

"*There are no such things as ghosts*," his mother said emphatically. "Now eat your supper, Jamie."

A gust of chilly air hit the back of Jamie's neck. Under the table Fireplug let out a whine. The kitchen door flew open, slamming against the sink with such force that a pane of glass broke. Then, just as quickly, it closed with a bang and shattered glass crashed to the floor.

Jamie's mother jumped up and ran to the door. "Oh, dear! Jamie, you'll have to close the door tighter when you come in so the wind doesn't blow it open. Now there's another job to be done." She stooped and picked up the larger pieces of glass. "Will you put a piece of cardboard over the opening, Jim? We don't want this cold wind coming in tonight."

Jamie stared. A shiver ran up his spine. He had closed the door tight when he came in. He *knew* he had!

CHAPTER EIGHT

"MORE THAN SIMPLE TRESPASSING"

Jamie pushed his breakfast cereal back and forth in the bowl. He wasn't very hungry this morning, but you can't sneak soggy corn flakes under the table. He glanced at the cardboard-covered window. The wind had been howling around the house when he had gone to his room last night, but he doubted it was the wind that had slammed the kitchen door open and shut.

"You'll have to go to school by yourself this morning," his mother said. "Your father and I are going to take Margaret to the orthodontist to get her braces adjusted. When you get home, do your chores and your homework and help yourself to whatever you want from the refrigerator. We'll try to get home early, but don't worry if we're a little late. You know how it gets with the city traffic."

"You leaving now?" Jamie asked. If they left before the school bus came, he could cut classes and hunt for

the hidden money.

"We'll leave after the bus picks you up," his mother answered.

"There'll be no hookey-playing here, young man." She hugged Jamie and gave him a kiss. "You promised you'd get good grades, remember?"

"Sure, Mom," Jamie replied, his voice barely able to disguise his disappointment. At times, it was almost as though his mother could read his mind!

When the horn on the school bus sounded outside the house, Jamie was ready.

"Your sister's not going in this morning?" Mr. Carter asked from his seat behind the wheel.

"No. She's going to the dentist today," Jamie answered. He passed the empty seat next to Chuck and sat behind him, next to Scooter.

"Dr. James doesn't open his office until after lunch," Scooter said. "That's so kids can see him after school, and he stays open late."

"Margaret doesn't go to him." Jamie replied. "Mom and Dad are taking her to the dentist in New York who's been straightening her teeth." Looking around secretively, Jamie whispered to Scooter, "Is there any way we can get off the bus before it gets to school?"

"Mr. Carter would report us if we did. Why?"

"Oh, I just thought it would be a good time to check out the secret passage. I don't feel like waiting 'til Saturday."

Scooter frowned as he looked toward Chuck sitting in front of them. He shook his head at Jamie and attempted to change the subject. "Get your homework done?" he asked in a loud voice.

Jamie grinned. "Sure did," he replied in a voice loud enough for Chuck to hear. "The old ghost helped me. Then he said he'd help me look for the treasure Saturday."

Before Scooter could answer, the bus stopped in front of the school and Mr. Carter opened the door. "Watch the steps," he warned.

Chuck jumped up before the bus stopped. He stumbled in his haste to get out, then ran toward the building. By the time Jamie and Scooter were off the bus, Chuck had disappeared.

"Sure in a hurry, isn't he?" Scooter said.

Jamie laughed. "Probably thought the ghost was after him."

"You'd better quit baiting him, Jamie." Scooter said. "He's mean when he wants to be—and that's most of the time."

"I'm not afraid of him," Jamie replied as the two prepared to go to their separate classrooms. "See you later, Scooter."

The hours crept by while Jamie waited impatiently for school to end. He was determined to explore the chimney when he got home. Waiting for Saturday was for the birds.

When the final bell rang, Jamie met Scooter on the bus. A new driver was behind the wheel instead of Mr. Carter. When he started to close the door, Scooter called out, "Wait! Chuck's not here yet."

The driver looked around. "He went home early; said he was sick."

"Some tough guy," Jamie said under his breath.

"If you'd rather not stay alone, you can come home with me, Jamie, "Scooter said.

"You think I'm scared to stay alone?"

" 'Course not. Only . . . well, old houses can be pretty spooky, you know,"

"Pooh!" Jamie scoffed. "If Elmer's a ghost, he's a pretty *tame* one. He's a nice old guy. I bet he's some kind of magician. Anyhow, he don't scare me none."

"If he's a magician, what's he doing hanging around your place? Seems kind of crazy to me," Scooter said.

Jamie didn't answer. He wanted to tell Scooter the rest, but it sounded too nutty. Whoever heard of a ghost being a private eye? Besides, Elmer wouldn't show himself when Scooter was around, so Scooter probably thought Jamie was imagining things, too. Well, he didn't need any help. He could tie the old rope ladder together where it had rotted through, knot it around the hook it had hung from, and lower himself down the chimney.

When Jamie got off the bus, Fireplug was nowhere to be seen. He looked around and whistled. Just as Jamie started to call his dog, he heard the hens squawking in the barn. What's going on there he wondered, stopping momentarily and looking in that direction. Was Fireplug chasing them? He did it once, when they had first gotten the chickens, and Jamie's father smacked him with a broom for it. Fireplug never had to be told twice not to do something, and Jamie's suspicions were aroused. Hastily dropping his school books in the front yard, Jamie hurried toward the barn.

Inside the door, Jamie blinked as he saw an old kerosene lantern on the floor. Its flickering flame cast eerie, wavering shadows in the dim light. Suddenly, a rough pair of hands grabbed Jamie, pinning his arms in a vise-like grip. Reacting quickly, Jamie began struggling, twisting his head to look up at his attacker. Towering over him was a tall, well-built man dressed in dark clothing. A black cloth bag with eye-holes cut out of it covered his head.

"Who are you?" Jamie asked, his voice quivering with the cold fear shooting through him.

"Never mind, kid!" the man growled. "Just tell me where the money's buried!"

"Get your hands off me!" Jamie shouted, struggling to free himself from the man's iron grasp. "Where's my dog?"

A long, drawn-out howl came faintly to his ears. "What'd you do to him?" Jamie demanded.

"Forget that old mutt, boy!" the man said, shaking Jamie. "Talk!"

"I don't know where the money is, and even if I did I wouldn't tell you," Jamie replied defiantly. "Now let go of me!"

A big hand slapped Jamie across the face. Jamie's city street instincts came quickly into play, and he kicked out as hard as he could. A startled curse came from beneath the black bag as Jamie's foot tore a painful gash in his attacker's shin. The hand still holding him loosened and Jamie was able to jerk himself free. In his backward lunge, he tripped over the lantern, knocking it over and sending it rolling through the straw. Before he could recover his balance, a heavy fist hit his nose, sending him backward. Jamie sprawled on the floor with stars circling before his eyes in crazy patterns.

Tears of pain welled up in his eyes but, through the blur, Jamie saw the intruder race out the door. The straw had caught fire and flames raced across the floor in all directions. Hens squawked in fear and confusion, and the rooster sounded an alarm, crowed from his perch. Another long, mournful howl reminded Jamie his dog was in trouble.

Struggling to his feet, Jamie used his sleeve to wipe away the blood dripping from his nose. He raced out of the burning barn, paused to listen. Frantic yips were coming from inside the well!

Quickly Jamie ran to look over the side of the well. Fireplug was in the water, his front paws paddling desperately to keep himself afloat.

"I'm right here, boy. Keep swimming," Jamie called down to him.

His hands worked swiftly as he lowered the big wooden bucket to the water, giving it more rope to get it within his dog's reach. Fireplug's paws caught the edge of the bucket, tilting it toward him so he could fall head first inside. Jamie pulled it up, turning the crank as fast as he could with both hands, and straining under its weight. When the bucket got within his reach, Jamie grabbed it and dumped dog and water on the grass.

Fireplug sprang to his feet and shook himself. He looked half-drowned and he was shivering, but otherwise appeared to be okay. Jamie picked him up and hugged him, thankful that his pet was uninjured. Blood from Jamie's nose dripped onto his dog's wet fur.

"Oh, Fireplug, you're all right!" Jamie gasped, out of breath and still in pain from the two blows to his head. Suddenly, remembering the burning barn, he looked toward it and saw the flames leaping higher.

"Oh, gosh, it's going up! I better call the fire department!"

He raced toward the house with Fireplug at his heels,

quickly unlocked the door, and made a beeline for the kitchen. Grabbing the telephone, he dialed the operator. When she answered he gave his name and address and told her their barn was burning. "I'll call the fire department immediately, sir," she said as she clicked off. Jamie hung up and grabbed his wet dog, dashing back outside.

Long minutes went by before sirens down the road announced the arrival of the volunteer fire department. The fire truck came first. It was followed by a string of cars with flashing blue lights that stopped a safe distance from the burning building. The truck rolled into the yard as close as it could get, and the volunteers on it jumped off and quickly began unraveling hoses from the pumper. The men coming from the cars ran over to the truck and helped train the hoses on the blaze.

The pump whined and whirred as it pushed a steady stream of water onto the flames, but it was too late. The fire was out of control. It had burned a hole in the roof, sending showers of sparks over the dry shingles. The raging blaze took great bites of the building as though it were some starving monster, and the entire structure was engulfed. When the supply of water began to run low, the truck moved back a safe distance. The firemen sprayed the ground around the barn to prevent the shower of sparks from spreading the flames. As the last few drops trickled out of the pumper, they stood around and watched the building sink in on itself. Beams crashed down into the flames. Old boards crumbled into ashes. The whole barn was now one big bonfire.

Jamie watched, his eyes horrified. Dad would be furious!

Amid the confusion, Scooter came running toward Jamie. "You okay, Jamie?" he asked in a frantic, worried voice. "Gosh, what happened?"

He turned as a woman came up behind him. "This is Jamie Boyd, Ma."

"Are you hurt, Jamie?" she asked. "Your folks aren't back yet? Land sakes! You and that dog are both soaked. Come into the house and dry off."

She urged Jamie toward the door of the kitchen. He stumbled ahead of her, dazed. Fireplug wriggled in his arms.

"Maybe we'd better leave the dog outside," Scooter's mother said.

"No," Jamie said, clutching the dog tighter. "He almost drowned."

Once inside, Mrs. Johnson sent Scooter to get towels from the bathroom. Fireplug wriggled loose and went to roll himself dry on the rug in front of the sink.

Scooter had just returned carrying two big towels when Jamie's parents raced through the door with Margaret close behind them.

"Jamie, are you all right?" they all asked at once.

Margaret grabbed one of the towels and wrapped it around him. The crisis made her lay aside her normal animosity toward her younger brother.

"Your nose is bleeding," his mother said. She dabbed at it with the other towel. "You're so wet! And your face . . . oh, dear, what happened to your face?"

"He might be in shock," Jim said. "Keep rubbing him with that towel, Margaret."

Scooter's mother handed her some ice cubes wrapped in a cloth. "This will stop the nosebleed, Mrs. Boyd."

Jamie's mother gently placed the ice on his nose. "Hold it there, Margaret. I think he's dry enough. You can stop rubbing now."

"Say something, Jamie," Margaret said. "How'd you get so beat up?"

Jamie blinked and his aching head began to clear. He pushed Margaret's hand away. "I'm okay."

"Are you sure, son?" Jim asked.

"Yes. I'm all right, Dad," Jamie said.

"Then, I'd better go see about the barn," Jim said. "We'll have time for explanations later." He raced out the door.

"Oh, dear!" Jamie's mother sighed, sinking into a nearby chair.

"Can I make some coffee or tea for you, Mrs. Boyd?" Scooter's mother asked. When Ellen looked up, she added, "I'm Martha Johnson—Scooter's mother."

"Oh, yes, we met at church." One hand went to her forehead.

"We saw the fire while we were all the way down the road, and I thought we'd never get here. I was afraid something had happened to Jamie."

"I'm all right, Mom," Jamie said.

"What happened, Jamie?"

Jamie sniffed and Margaret wiped a drop of blood from the end of his nose. When he frowned, she laughed. "Yeah, he's all right, Mom."

"Tell me what happened, Jamie," his mother repeated impatiently.

"Some guy threw Fireplug down the well and grabbed me when I went into the barn."

"Who?"

"I don't know, Mom. He had a bag over his head. He asked me where the money was hidden, and I told him I didn't know. Then he smacked me and I kicked him in the leg. I got away from him, but I tripped over the lantern he'd set down. Then he hit me in the nose and ran off. I *had* to get Fireplug out of the water, and then I phoned the operator. By that time the fire was too big to stop. I'm sorry, Mom."

"Oh, Jamie, I don't care about the barn. I was scared out of my wits for *you*. I thought you might have been killed. I wish we'd never seen this place!" she said, getting up to put her arms around him.

"Aaah, Mom, I'm not a baby," Jamie said glancing over at Scooter. "Me and Fireplug can take care of ourselves, but this guy sure fouled things up!"

"We'd better go home," Mrs. Johnson said. "Is there anything else I can do before we go, Mrs. Boyd?"

"You've done plenty, Mrs. Johnson," Ellen replied. "I can't thank you enough for helping Jamie. As soon as things quiet down, I'd like you and your family to come over for dinner one day."

"Are you sure you're all right now?"

"Yes, I'm fine." She glanced at Margaret. "I have a good daughter to help me."

When Scooter and his mother had gone, Ellen sank limply back into her chair. "Oh, dear!" she said, sighing again.

Jamie stood up. "Gee, Mom, you sure look pale. Can I get you some water or something?"

He heard the sound of starting cars and shouts of goodbye outside. He wanted to see what was happening, but his mother looked too funny.

"Mom?" Jamie repeated.

"Go on if you want, Jamie," Margaret said. "I'll fix some tea."

The words were hardly out of her mouth when Jim entered with the sheriff beside him.

"Well, the barn's gone," Jim announced. "Are you all okay in here? Jamie, what's that bruise on your cheek?"

"Aaah . . . that's where the guy belted me, Dad."

"What guy?" Jim demanded. "I want to hear the whole story, son. How did the fire get started?"

Sheriff Griffith stepped forward authoritatively. "Maybe I'd better hear this, too, Jamie. Tell us what happened, and take your time."

Jamie repeated the story he told his mother, adding a few details he'd left out before.

"Was it the old man you've been telling us about?" his father asked.

"No, Dad. I don't know who it was, but I'd know his voice if I heard it again. Look, I'm sorry about the barn."

"So am I, Jamie, but it's more important to me that *you're* safe. It doesn't sound like it was your fault."

He looked at the sheriff. "Is there any way you can find out who attacked my son and burned our barn, Sheriff Griffith?" Jim asked.

Before the sheriff could answer, Fireplug came over and pushed at Jim's hand with his nose. "And find out who threw Jamie's dog in the well, too."

"I'll sure try, Mr. Boyd. Looks like we've got *a lot* of investigating to do," the sheriff said.

"Tomorrow I'm going to close the top on that well and put a pump on it," Jim continued. "An open hole like that is dangerous." Anger began rising in his voice.

"What kind of a sick person would hit a kid and try to drown his dog?"

The sheriff put a hand on Jamie's shoulder. "Probably the same kind of man who killed Mathieson's dog first, and then killed old Mathieson. Could be that we're dealing with the same person here."

Jamie moved from under the sheriff's hand. "Did you find out who owned that knife yet?"

"No, Jamie, but I will," he replied. "We're still investigating it. That's an unusual knife, and we're asking around. We expect somebody to recognize it one of these days." He paused. "You say you'd know the voice again if you heard it?"

"Well . . . I don't know for sure. He might have been doing something to make it sound different," Jamie answered. "But I can prove it was him by the marks."

"What marks?" the sheriff asked.

"The ones I put on his shin. I really kicked him good," Jamie said proudly.

"Well, I can't go around asking every man in town to pull up his pant legs," Sheriff Griffith said, "but if you hear that voice again, you let me know immediately."

"What happens if somebody finds the money before we do?" Jamie blurted out.

Everybody looked at him when he asked the question, but it was the sheriff who answered.

"Now, Jamie, I doubt there is any money," he said. "I think that story got started the way all ghost yarns do. Stories like that get bigger with each telling."

"But what if there *is* ten thousand dollars buried out there somewhere?" Jamie persisted.

The sheriff smiled. "Well, it seems to me it would be

finders keepers. If the money isn't stolen, and nobody can legally prove it's theirs, I guess whoever finds it will have a claim to it. Although the owner of the property could contest it, and it would be up to a judge to decide."

"I don't think you ought to worry about it tonight, son" Jamie's mother said. "Your eye has turned green, and now you have another bruise on your cheek. Oh, Jamie, you look terrible! Has your nose stopped bleeding?"

"Sure, Mom, it's okay." Jamie's mind was on the sheriff's words more than his own discomfort. If the man who grabbed him in the barn was still prowling around, *he* might find the money first. Then it would be *his*! What if he came into the house and discovered the opening in the chimney? Elmer came and went at will, so that meant others could get into the house as well. Maybe the man had come inside while everybody was watching the fire! He might be snooping around in the attic right now!

"Jamie!" his mother called.

"What, Mom? Were you talking to me? I didn't hear you."

"Oh, dear!" she said, her voice growing worried. "Perhaps that blow deafened you in one ear."

"It didn't, Mom. I was just thinking about something. I can hear you okay."

"Well, I said you'd better eat something and then go to bed," she said. Her body shuddered uncontrollably for a few seconds. "I won't sleep a wink if someone's sneaking around this farm."

"Don't worry, Mrs. Boyd," the sheriff said. "Whoever set the fire and attacked Jamie is probably long gone. He's not going to hang around with all these people coming out here. But I'd keep my eyes and ears open at all times.

Whoever it was will probably be back if he thinks that money is around. You might want to double lock all your doors, and call me the minute you suspect any trouble," he added grimly.

"We'll do that, sheriff," Jim said. "Thank you for all your help."

"Sorry you lost your barn, Mr. Boyd, but if we find out who did it, he may have more than just a simple trespassing and property destruction rap on his hands. He's going to have a lot of other questions to answer, also. And we'll make sure he pays you for a new barn. Now, you call me if there's anymore trouble, you hear?"

After adjusting his gun belt, the sheriff left, carefully closing the door with the cardboard-covered window.

"What a day!" Jim exclaimed. "It looks like more rain tonight, so that will finish putting out the fire."

"Are you hungry, Jim?" Ellen asked.

"No, thanks. It's a good thing we had supper in town, the way things turned out."

"Did the chickens get out in time?" she asked.

"I think so, honey," he said nodding his head. "Hens are smarter than people think when it comes to self-preservation. They're probably out roosting in the trees. I heard the rooster crow a few times, so we know he got out in time. Tomorrow when it's light, we'll go out there and gather them up. We don't need a big barn, anyway. I'll just build a chicken coop, and it will be a lot easier to keep up."

He sighed with exhaustion. It had been a long day for him, driving to and from the city, and then coming home to a fire and an assault on his son. "I'm just glad the fire didn't spread to the house," he said, ruffling Jamie's hair.

"You look like you've been through the war, son. If you don't feel like going to school tomorrow, you can take a day off to rest."

"Thanks, Dad." Jamie pushed back from the table. "I think I'll turn in. Fireplug and me had a crazy day."

"Fireplug and *I*," his mother corrected. "I'll be up in a few minutes, honey."

After Jamie's mother had made her usual bedtime visit, Jamie waited until the house grew quiet. This time he forced his eyes to remain open. He was tired, but more determined than ever to check out the secret passage.

He walked quietly over to the window and looked out. The remains of the barn were still smoldering, but the few flickering embers that glowed in the dark posed no further danger. The stars that usually shone so brightly were screened by the smoke and a thick bank of low-hanging clouds.

Rain began to fall, further blurring the view as it hit the window. Jamie returned to the bed and patted Fireplug.

"I'm going to leave you here for awhile, boy," he whispered. "You be quiet so Mom doesn't come, you hear?"

Jamie pulled his jeans over his pajama bottoms and slipped into his sneakers. Tiptoeing to the door, Jamie listened for several seconds before he opened it. The hall was empty.

Fireplug bounded down from the bed and raced to the door, but Jamie quickly closed it. "Get back to bed, boy!" Jamie commanded.

The little dog sat down and stared at Jamie, one paw raised. "Go on," Jamie insisted.

The shaggy head cocked to one side, and Jamie sighed. He had made fun of Scooter's dog obeying each order when it was given, but it sure would be nice if old Fireplug would mind just once in a while.

Jamie quickly opened the door and slipped through. He heard Fireplug scratch and whispered, "Sssh." The scratching stopped.

At the door to the third floor, Jamie stopped to listen again. The rain beat steadily against the old house, but otherwise it was quiet. He slowly opened the door and the hinges squeaked. Carefully, he closed it behind him and walked up the dusty steps.

The shaky old ladder was still in place with its top stuck into the trap door leading to the attic. Jamie tiptoed past the closed doors along the hall and climbed the ladder, hoping the sound of the rain would cover up any noise he might make. The one thing he didn't want to do was wake his parents.

The attic was so dark he could hardly see. Why hadn't he thought to bring a flashlight? Oh, well, he could feel his way around the junk until he got to the chimney. It was lucky they hadn't replaced the heavy panel. He might not be able to get it out by himself.

The room wasn't very cold, so Elmer must not be around. Funny how the old man brought such ice-cold air with him whenever he showed up. Maybe he really *was* a ghost. Jamie grinned, thinking about his mother. If there were such things as ghosts, wouldn't she be surprised?

He felt his way around on the rough bricks, and his hands guided him to the big hole in the chimney. The old rope ladder was inside. He straightened it out by feeling it blindly in the dark, and knotted the pieces together. Oily dirt encrusted the rope, and it was thin and ragged in spots, but he figured it would hold his light weight. Hadn't it held grown men at one time?

When he was finished, Jamie got up and tied the ladder around the hook inside the chimney. Then he gathered up the rest and lowered it down the flue where it dangled perilously.

Rain beat against the old roof, and Jamie shivered. He wasn't afraid of the dark, but it was pretty spooky to go down a narrow shaft into . . . what? What was down there? He couldn't see much inside the black chimney. Now he wished he had brought Fireplug along, but he knew any barking would wake his parents.

With his heart pounding furiously, Jamie sat on the edge of the opening, grabbed the rope with both hands and swung his feet inside. He carefully placed one foot on the top rung, then went down foot under foot into the mysterious secret passage below.

It was slow going with the ladder swinging so unsteadily. Several times he let go of the rope with one hand to brush away the webs that stuck to his face. His arms ached and his legs began to cramp. He wondered how deep the hole below him was.

The old rope creaked under the strain. It squeaked against the iron hook above when Jamie's weight shifted. Something crawled on his neck and he swiped at it with one hand. The extra strain must have been too much. Suddenly Jamie felt the rope give way. He was falling!

He clawed wildly at the walls, reaching for something to break his fall, but no handhold came within his blind grasp. Webs and soot mashed against his face as he plunged down the old flue. With a last, desperate effort, Jamie pulled himself into as tight a ball as he could. When he hit the bottom of the shaft, the impact knocked him cold.

CHAPTER NINE

TRAPPED

A pain like none Jamie had ever felt brought him back to consciousness. He choked and gagged, gulping like a fish as he tried to draw air into empty lungs. Tears came to his eyes. His heart was racing madly. He gasped until healing oxygen finally let him breathe again. He drew in deep mouthfuls of air, spitting and sputtering out spider webs, dust, and old fireplace ashes.

At last he could sit up. It was too dark to see anything. His hands felt rags mixed with the dirt he had landed on. It must be some long-unused landing pad for the runaway slaves coming down the rope ladder many years earlier.

Jamie's head spun and his back throbbed. Tears ran slowly down his cheeks. He felt more miserable than he ever had in his life. Now he was *scared*!

"Oh, gee," he moaned.

He was down in this hole with no way to get out. *Nobody* knew where he was—not even Fireplug! Insects

101

he couldn't see crawled over him in the darkness. He knew most spiders were harmless, but some had mean bites that were poisonous. And what if there were snakes down here? A chill crossed Jamie's aching back. He didn't mind things he could see, but being blind in the dark—that was different.

"It's a mess, isn't it?" an eerie voice said out of the darkness.

Jamie jumped up, startled. Goose bumps rose on his arms. The hair on the back of his neck stood on end.

"Did it to yourself, didn't you?" the voice continued. Then a ghostly glow appeared with Elmer shimmering in its midst.

"You *are* a ghost!" Jamie's voice squeaked on the last word.

"I've been telling you that all along, boy. I was beginning to think you were stupid. Now I'm sure of it." Elmer sat on his heels and grinned. "Came down sort of fast, didn't you?"

Jamie shivered and tried to scrunch lower in his pajama top. "Why's it always so cold when you're around?" he asked.

"Something about my metabolism, I think. I ain't got none." Elmer chuckled at his own joke. Then he got serious. "Didn't break anything, did you? Arm? Leg? Neck?"

"I'm sore all over, but I don't think I broke anything," Jamie replied. In spite of his pain, he sniffed back his tears and tried to smile. "That last step down was a *long* one!" Like Elmer, he grinned at his own feeble joke.

"Uh-huh," Elmer agreed. "How come you didn't bring a light?"

"I didn't think about it."

"Don't think about much, do you? You knew that old rope was rotten."

"Yeah . . . but I thought it would hold me. I don't weigh all that much." Jamie groaned as he shifted his position. "Hey, with you giving off that light, maybe we can see if that money's down here. How come you didn't shine like that before?"

"Takes a lot of energy to glow like I'm doing now." Elmer's voice was grumpy. "Makes my arthritis worse, too, I think, so don't count on me playing lantern for you very long."

Jamie snickered. "You look like a Halloween pumpkin."

"Well, you act like one," the old man countered. "Pumpkins are brainless and people aren't. Or at least they *shouldn't* be."

"Aaah, I use my brains when I have to," Jamie replied defensively.

Elmer snorted. "Oh, *sure* you do. You let other people do your thinking more often than you bother to do it yourself."

"What do you mean?"

"Figure it out for yourself. What happened in New York to get you in trouble with the police?"

"Aaah, the fuzz were always chasing us away from some place or other," Jamie grumbled. "Everyone gets in trouble in the city."

"I don't mean that," Elmer said. "What did you get busted for?"

"Ripping off a ball."

"And why did you steal the ball?"

"The gang dared me to," Jamie answered.

The old man sat silent in the flickering light.

"Ours went down a sewer," Jamie added. He thought for a minute and then said, "Guess it really *wasn't* my idea, was it?"

"You've already answered your own question, boy," Elmer replied. "And, when you're in school, you wait to see how the other boys act before you decide how you want to behave. Why don't you think for yourself?"

Elmer frowned at him and continued. "Even though I appeared and disappeared right before your eyes and *told* you I was a ghost, you still didn't believe it. Just because your mother told you there were no ghosts, you wouldn't even think for yourself whether she was right or not."

The old ghost's glow had changed from pale yellow to orange as he grew more excited. Now it flickered to a red glare and his voice got louder. "Use the brain God gave you! Don't let it get flabby from lack of use. It's the most important organ in your whole body!"

Elmer's heavy eyebrows were drawn together. As his eerie halo grew redder, he looked almost like the devil himself. Jamie's eyes widened as he watched the old ghost's display of temper.

"I'm sorry," Jamie said meekly. His voice shook.

"Being sorry doesn't cut any ice," Elmer snapped. The red glow began to pale into yellow. "That is, unless it teaches you not to be stupid."

He winced as he slowly arose. "My bunions hurt!" he sighed blowing out a gust of icy air. "Try to stand up, boy. We'd better see if there's a way out of here for you. I can go anywhere I want, but you can't."

"Can't you make me disappear and take me with you?"

"Now, *that's* a stupid question!" Elmer said. "Think about it."

Jamie toyed with the idea, and then he nodded. "I guess I have to be dead before I can disappear like you do."

"*Now* you're getting the idea. Think things out for yourself. Don't open your mouth just to let out a lot of noise. Can you get up?"

Jamie held out his hand. "Help me."

"How?" Elmer demanded. He held out his arm. "Try to take it."

Jamie reached for Elmer's arm and his hand passed right through it. He tried again, but had the same result. Although he could see the old man, there was nothing to touch. Beads of cold sweat dotted his forehead.

"Now don't get scared, Jamie." Elmer said. "Think! Have I hurt you in any way?"

Jamie shook his head.

"Then don't panic." Elmer took a step backward. "Get up on your own."

Every bone in his body hurt as Jamie pushed himself to his feet. He hadn't known there were so many places that could ache. "Owww! My back hurts," he complained.

"Yeah, and when you get some age on you, it'll hurt even more. Especially if arthritis sets in," Elmer said. "Arthritis gets into your weakest parts, though, so it'll most likely land in your head. Come on now; I can only shine a little longer."

Jamie followed Elmer down the narrow tunnel. Wooden beams held the ceiling up, but dirt lay in piles where the braces had rotted with age. The tunnel grew narrower and more cramped. Finally, Elmer stopped and his glow dimmed.

"We've got a slide blocking us, Jamie. I have to quit shining or my knees will buckle, but we can feel our way back."

Jamie saw that the tunnel was closed off with dirt from floor to roof. When Elmer's light flickered out, they were left in darkness again.

Cold air passed over Jamie as Elmer went by. "Come on, boy," he said. "Maybe you can holler loud enough to be heard. Every time I try to yell, my throat gives me trouble."

Jamie trudged along thinking about what Elmer had said. He hadn't thought of his brain as an organ! In fact, he wasn't real sure what a brain looked like. Maybe he could look it up in the library.

Suddenly Jamie stopped. "Hey, Elmer, we forgot to look for the money."

"Think, Jamie," the voice said from the darkness ahead. "Do you really believe any human has been down here recently? I can pass through spider webs without breaking them, but people can't."

Jamie sighed. "I should've known that when I saw all the webs. I guess it saves a lot of trouble if you think things through before you shoot off your mouth."

"Right!"

There was silence for a time as Jamie walked slowly through the tunnel. He wondered how long he'd be down here. Forever?

"If you'll think back, Jamie, you might even remember a clue you passed over that could tell you where something is hidden," Elmer said.

"What clue? What did I miss?"

Elmer chuckled. "There you go again—wanting me to do your thinking. If you can't remember it, maybe one of these days I'll give you a hint. I'd like to get this case solved so I can go home, you know."

Jamie walked right into the wall of the chimney base. He groaned, stepping back as he rubbed his forehead.

"Why didn't you stop me, Elmer?"

"Why didn't you stop yourself?" the old man answered. "Try yelling up the chimney." He snickered. "I've heard of hollering down a rain barrel, but that gets you nothing."

"Help!" Jamie yelled at the top of his lungs. He repeated it several times. His cries filled the shaft, but there was no echo. The bricks muffled the sound.

"You should have fallen down a brass bell," Elmer said, then chuckled.

"I'm thirsty."

"Yelling'll make you that way," Elmer said. "Guess we'd better wait until morning. Your folks will miss you and start looking. Maybe you can make enough noise so they'll find you."

"You sure make it cold down here."

"Want me to leave?"

"No," Jamie said quickly.

"Well, let's get some sleep then," Elmer said. "I'll go down the tunnel a ways so you'll be warmer."

"You won't leave, will you?" Jamie asked fearfully.

"Heck, no," the old man answered. "This is the first time any human who knows I'm a ghost has wanted me to hang around. It's sort of nice."

Jamie huddled in a corner of the cold, dark shaft, wishing he'd worn a sweater or coat. The wind outside had shifted, and now raindrops were falling on his nose. He pressed against the wall to escape the rain coming in from above, but it did him little good. What a dope he had been! What he wouldn't give to have Fireplug with him!

He thought of his parents. His mother was so nice and warm. Dad had always been on his side when the cops came to report him, even if he did give lectures after they left. Jamie sighed. He deserved those lectures.

Even Margaret wouldn't be so bad to have with him right now. She really was okay as sisters go. If he'd stop riding her every chance he got, maybe she wouldn't get so mad at him.

He tried to move closer to the wall. Streaks of pain shot through him. Now he would have even more bruises to add to the ones on his eye and cheek.

As the long night passed, the rain gradually stopped coming down the chimney. Jamie stuck his head under the opening and stared upward. Was the sky getting light? Gosh, he wished daylight would hurry up and come.

From a distance he heard barking and his heart leaped with joy. Fireplug! His dog had found him!

Jamie struggled to his feet and began shouting. "Hey, boy, down here! Help! Fireplug! Down here, boy!"

"Jamie! Are you down there?" His father's voice traveled down the flue like a blast of warm air. "Jamie?"

"I'm stuck here, Dad!" Jamie called back. "The rope broke and I can't get back up. The tunnel's blocked."

Jamie heard Fireplug's wild barking and a sense of relief passed through him. His nightmare was over.

"Are you hurt?" his father called down to him.

"I'm okay. Just get me out of here, huh?"

"I'll have to get a rope, son. Be right back."

"Gosh, Jamie, are you scared?" Margaret's voice replaced his father's. "Did you fall very far?"

He started to give his sister a smart answer, but thought better of it. "Pretty far, I guess, but nothing's broken. Gee, I'm glad you found me."

"I heard Fireplug barking up a storm," Margaret said. "I got up to see what was wrong, and when I looked in your room he ran right past me to the upstairs door. When he started scratching at it I knew you were up there and I woke Dad. Mom's worried sick. Oh, here she is now."

"Jamie?" his mother called. "Are you hurt?"

"I'm okay, Mom. Elmer's down here with me." He tried to look down the black tunnel. "You still there, Elmer?"

There was no answer. The tunnel had grown much warmer.

"At least he was," Jamie added, almost to himself.

"What? I can't hear you, Jamie. What did you say?"

"I wish I was out of here, Mom," Jamie called up the chimney.

"Your father is coming, honey. Oh, dear, I wish you'd look before you leap into things." Her voice sounded tired.

"I will, Mom. Hurry up with that rope, Dad."

"Stand back, son," his father ordered.

Jamie stepped backward and waited. A coil of rope landed in front of him.

"Tie a loop in the end of it, Jamie, and make sure the knot is tight. Put your foot in the loop and hang onto the rope with both hands while we pull you up."

When Jamie had done what his father told him, he called, "Okay, Dad. I'm ready."

The line pulled him upward while he held on tight. He bumped against the sooty walls and swung back and forth like a pendulum. It was painful but he continued to hang on. When his head reached the opening in the chimney, his father grabbed him while Margaret and his mother kept the rope taut.

Jamie almost fell as he came out of the chimney, but his father held onto him.

"Good Lord, Jamie, are you all in one piece?" his father asked.

"Oh, Jamie," his mother wailed.

Margaret started to laugh.

Jamie sheepishly faced his family. He saw the black smears on his father's pajamas. "Gosh, I got you all dirty, Dad!"

He turned to his mother, expecting her to hug him, but she stepped backward, leaning against the wall. Margaret was doubled up with laughter.

Jamie was bewildered. "What's so funny?"

"You," Margaret gasped. "You should see yourself!"

Jamie's father grinned. "You're as filthy a boy as I've ever seen. What made you dive into that dirty old chimney? I told you we'd look for the other end this Saturday, didn't I?"

Jamie looked his father in the eye. "I just didn't think, Dad. I couldn't wait." He glanced at his mother and sister. "I'm sorry I gave you all so much trouble."

They stared at him, and Jamie decided he had been sorry enough.

"I hurt, Mom," he said. "I hurt everywhere there's a place to hurt."

His mother started toward the trap door. "I just bet

you do, young man. First thing you get is a hot bath, and *then* I'll get close enough to fix your wounds."

Jim winked at Jamie and motioned him to follow his mother. With a sigh of relief, Jamie went after her.

CHAPTER TEN

THE SEARCH GOES ON

After a warm bath, Jamie went to bed. His mother brought a tray with hot soup that chased the last chill from his insides. Fireplug snuggled as close to Jamie as he could, happy to have him back. Jamie shuddered as he remembered the cold darkness of the chimney pit. His back hurt, his arms and legs ached, and even his head throbbed with pain.

"Maybe I should get a doctor to look you over," his mother said.

"Nothing's broken, Mom. Honest," Jamie replied, putting on a brave front.

"Well, I'll give you some aspirin, anyway. It will ease the pain."

His mother returned with a glass of water and two aspirin tablets. Jamie washed them down with a big drink of water.

"Now go to sleep," she ordered. She sat in the chair

Elmer had used. "I'll just sit here a while and watch over you."

"Aw, Mom. . ."

Jamie started to protest, then stopped. It was sort of nice to have his mother around. His eyes closed as the throbbing of his body ceased, and Jamie slept.

When he awoke, it was dim in his room and outside the window. It was almost dark. Had he slept the day away? Jamie turned on the lamp and looked around. His mother was gone.

The aching started again when Jamie moved, but he forced himself stiffly out of bed. With Fireplug bounding along beside him, he went down to the kitchen.

"Hi," he said.

Scooter and Margaret were sitting at the table with his Dad. His mother looked around from where she was working at the stove.

"Hi, yourself," she said. "I thought you'd sleep around the clock and starve before you woke up. We were just getting ready to eat supper."

"You find any treasure yet?" Scooter asked, grinning at him. "Chuck was back at school today, and when you didn't show up, he asked me where you were."

"Mr. Carter must still be sick," Margaret said. "That new bus driver is nice, but he drives worse than Mr. Carter did. He jerks the bus every time he stops and starts."

Jamie took a chair at the table and waited while his mother set a plate and silverware in front of him. "What did you tell Chuck?" he asked Scooter.

"Nothing. Margaret told me what happened, but she said to just tell everyone you weren't feeling good." He stopped and looked Jamie over. "I guess you *aren't*, with all those scrapes and bruises. Why didn't you wait til I could help you?"

" 'Cause I'm dumb," Jamie said glumly. "How come your Mom let you come over on a week night?"

"This is 4-H night," Scooter answered. "I phoned Ma and asked her if I could go with Margaret. Do you want to go?"

"I'm driving," his father said. "If you feel up to it, son, we'll wait until you get dressed."

Jamie shook his head. "No. I'm hungry. I'll stay home with Mom. Maybe next time."

Car headlights flashed through the window, and everyone looked up. His father rose and went to the door.

"It's Sheriff Griffith," Jim announced. "Maybe he's found our barn burner." He opened the door and let him in. "Had dinner yet, sheriff?" he asked.

The sheriff nodded. "Yes, thanks. Everything quiet out here?" He looked at Jamie. "Hey, what happened to you, son? You tangle with somebody again?"

"Just a chimney this time, sheriff." Jim laughed, then went on to tell about Jamie's fall.

Sheriff Griffith shook his head as he heard the story. "Wish I was young enough to bounce back," he said. "A fall like that would about finish me, I expect."

"Find any clues on who burned our barn?" Jim asked.

"No, not yet," the sheriff admitted. "But strange things are happening and I don't know whether they're tied in with this Mathieson business or not. Dan Carter has disappeared. His daughter said he didn't come home yesterday. Since his wife died, Dan's been visiting a lot with another old bachelor, Jack Steward, and Jan figured he was with him. But when Dan still wasn't home this morning, she went looking for him at Jack's place. Jack hadn't seen him, so she came to tell me about it."

"Mr. Carter told the principal he was sick Tuesday morning when he brought the school bus in," Margaret said.

The sheriff smiled. "Dan's been known to sneak off and go hunting. Jan hates him killing animals, so he doesn't tell her when he's going. But he's never stayed this long." He paused, then added, "Jamie, could the voice you heard in the barn have been that of Dan Carter?"

Jamie swallowed the mouthful of food he was chewing before he could answer. "I don't think so," he said doubtfully. "But he talked funny and could have changed his voice, I guess."

"Why would Dan Carter be involved?" Jamie's father asked.

"Well, he and Jan have had a hard time since Mrs. Carter passed away. She had a lot of big medical bills, and driving a school bus doesn't pay very much. I thought people had given up on the money that's supposed to be buried out here, but as long as there's any hope of it, I guess they won't. I was just wondering if Dan might have been looking for it when Jamie came in, although why he'd be so secretive about it is beyond me."

Jamie clapped a hand over his mouth and everybody turned to look at him. "Me and my big mouth!" he exclaimed.

"What do you mean, Jamie?" his father asked.

"Aaah . . I was teasing Chuck Magruder on the bus by telling him I knew where the money was buried. Mr. Carter probably heard me."

"Well, let's not jump to conclusions," the sheriff said.

"We can't accuse anybody of anything until we have proof. Dan might have a good explanation for why he's been gone."

"Did you find out who owned that knife yet, sheriff?" Jamie asked.

"Not yet, son. I've been showing it to everybody I can, hoping it will be recognized. The handle was hand-carved, so it most likely belonged to a whittler."

"Was Carter a whittler?" Jamie's father asked.

Scooter giggled. "Everybody's a whittler around here, Mr. Boyd. Even my Pa picks up a piece of wood and starts cutting whenever he sits down to talk to anybody—at least, when he's outside. Ma won't let him make a mess in the house."

Sheriff Griffith nodded. "That's right, son, but if that knife belongs to someone around here, sooner or later it will be recognized. Whittlers know each other's work as well as they know their own."

"Can't you send it to a crime lab to be examined?" Jim asked.

"It's too late for that," the sheriff explained. "It's been in the ground too long and we could never get any fingerprints off it."

Jamie's father glanced at the clock. "It's time we started for the meeting if we don't want to be late. Sure you don't want to go along, Jamie?"

"No thanks, Dad."

"I'd better get back, too," the sheriff said, heading for the door. "Let me know if anyone comes prowling around here again."

When everybody but his mother had gone, Jamie resumed eating. He had gotten so hungry while he was down the chimney, he doubted he would ever get filled up.

"Want anything else, honey?" his mother asked after Jamie had cleaned off his plate.

"No, Mom." Jamie got up and gave his mother a hug. "Gee, I'm sure glad you're here."

She returned the hug and then stood back to take a good look at him. "What happened to you while you were in that chimney, son? You're acting different since we pulled you up."

"Guess I thought about a lot of things, Mom."

"Tell me about it."

"Well, that old man I told you about showed up."

"Now, Jamie. Don't start *that* again."

"Honest, Mom! He's really a ghost. He glowed so we could see, and he let me try to feel his arm, and it wasn't there!" Jamie's words rushed out as he tried to tell the whole story before his mother could make him stop.

She listened, but there was still disbelief on her face. "You really believe all this, Jamie?"

"It sort of made sense, Mom. The way Elmer told me, I mean."

His mother sat down. "Well, it's quite a story," she said slowly. "You *are* growing up, and *should* think things out for yourself. I've never seen a ghost and I don't believe they exist. But I could be wrong," she added.

"You'd like Elmer, Mom," Jamie said with a grin. "He's tired and creaky, but he can't go home until we find out who killed Mr. Mathieson."

His mother returned the smile, but said nothing. She watched Fireplug creep out from under the table with the black iron ring he'd found in his mouth. "What's that he's carrying, Jamie?"

Jamie reached down to his dog and removed the ring from his mouth. As he examined it, his eyes widened.

"Mom! This is the same kind of ring that's in the chimney panel! I didn't think about it when Fireplug found it under the grain bin the other day, but now it makes sense! Maybe the other end of the tunnel comes out inside the barn."

"Well, there is no barn left," his mother pointed out. "And if the hens laid any eggs today, they're scattered out there in the grass."

"I'll get dressed and go hunt for the eggs, Mom."

"No, Jamie. You've been through enough for one day and besides, it's too dark to see anything."

"Aw, please, Mom? I've got to find the other end of that tunnel. Now that the barn's gone, it should be easy. Please?"

His mother opened her mouth as if to say something, then closed it. They stared at each other, and she smiled. "Well, why not?" she said finally. "Put some warm clothes on and I'll get a coat. We'll go hunting together. Now, where did Jim put that flashlight?"

Jamie started to run, but a shooting pain in his legs slowed him down. He walked up the stairs instead of taking them two at a time. Everything on his body hurt when he tried to get into his clothes, but he ignored the pain in his eagerness to continue the search.

"That dumb old rope," he grumbled, and then stopped. It wasn't the rope that was dumb.

When he returned to the kitchen, his mother was waiting. She held the flashlight out to Jamie. "You take the light and I'll follow you. You're the detective in this family."

"If the guy I tangled with hadn't been so big, I'd have sworn it was Chuck Magruder," Jamie said. "Every time he sees me he tries to pick a fight."

"It could have been anybody, Jamie. You heard the sheriff say you need proof before you can accuse someone." She picked up the egg basket. "Just in case."

Jamie noticed the glass was back in the door window. "I closed the door tight the other night, Mom. Honest! I think Elmer got mad when he heard what you were saying and slammed the door when he left."

His mother sighed. "Ghosts that are private investigators and glow in the dark . . . appear and disappear and tell you to think for yourself . . . make the air icy when they enter, and slam doors when they leave . . ." She sighed again. "It's going to take a while to make me believe all that, Jamie."

"Let's go, Mom." Jamie opened the door and went outside.

The night was pitch black. An acrid stench of charred old wood still hung over the farm. Clouds hid the stars and moon. Fireplug disappeared as he left the ring of light supplied by the flashlight in Jamie's hand.

Ashes were all that remained of the big old barn. The rain had turned them into a soggy cover on the ground. Jamie played the beam of light back and forth, trying to figure out where everything had been before the fire.

"Fireplug found that ring under the grain bin with the other stuff, Mom. Maybe the end of the tunnel is there."

"Now why would anybody dig a tunnel so it came up under a wooden bin?"

"Maybe it *didn't* come up under the bin," Jamie said slowly. "Maybe the bin was put over it to hide the opening. Gee, I wish we could see better."

"Perhaps we should wait until morning."

"Aw, gee, Mom; everything's always being put off. Can't we look now while we're already out here?" He flashed the light toward her so he could see.

His mother blinked and then smiled. "I guess we'd better, if it will keep you from jumping down any more holes by yourself. But let's go back and get the rake so we can move this mess without dirtying our hands."

"I'll get it, Mom. You wait right here." Jamie aimed the light ahead of him so he wouldn't stumble over anything on his way back to the house. Sore as he was, he sure didn't want to hit the ground again.

His father had stored their tools in a room next to the kitchen. It took Jamie only a moment to find the rake. He was on his way back out the door when he heard Fireplug's frantic barking. *Now* what had his dog discovered?

He hoped it wasn't a skunk. Scooter warned him you had to teach your dog not to go after a skunk, or else you'd spend days trying to wash the smell out of his fur.

"Fireplug! Come here!" he called.

A yelp of pain replaced the barking. Jamie broke into a run.

"Mom? What's happening?" he shouted.

CHAPTER ELEVEN

THE PROWLER RETURNS

The barking started again. In the light Jamie saw a black-clad form holding his mother, who was frantically trying to free herself. One big hand was clamped over her mouth to keep her from shouting.

Fireplug tried to bite the attacker, but the man's big boots were too thick. The little dog dodged to avoid another kick.

"Let her go!" Jamie shouted. He dropped the rake and rushed at his mother's attacker. A big boot caught him in the stomach. Jamie fell backward, groaning when he hit the ground.

"Grab your dog and keep him away," the man's voice rasped over the noise. "Tell me where the money's buried, or your mother's going to get hurt, boy."

Jamie's mother moaned when the hand left her mouth. "We don't know where any money's buried," she gasped. "Who *are* you?"

Jamie picked himself up and ignored the tears of pain that came to his eyes. "You might as well take that sack off your head," he said angrily. "We found the knife you used to kill Mathieson's dog, and Sheriff Griffith will soon find out who you are."

"You're a smart one, aren't you?" the voice growled. "Well, just remember . . . if I killed one mutt, I can just as easily get rid of another." He kicked at the charging Fireplug again. "Now, keep him away or I'll throw him down the well for good this time!"

Jamie grabbed Fireplug. "Let go my mother!" he demanded.

She cried out in pain as the man jerked her arms behind her. With a howl of rage Jamie let go of his dog, lowered his head, and charged. Again a boot sent him sprawling. Painfully he scrambled to his feet. Fireplug barked furiously, but stayed out of range.

"Shut up!" the voice ordered. "Keep that mutt quiet, boy! I'm not gonna tell you again!"

Jamie grabbed his dog and tried to quiet him, but without success. Suddenly a chilly breeze swirled around them and the air turned icy. Fireplug stopped barking. His ears flew skyward. He broke from Jamie's grasp and dashed toward the house. Jamie looked around, trying to peer into the darkness.

His mother cried out again and Jamie made up his mind. "Let her go," he repeated. "I'll tell you what I know, but it ain't much."

"Tell me first, and then I'll let her go."

Jamie looked at his mother and she nodded. Jamie took a deep breath. "Well, there's a secret tunnel from the attic down the chimney that's blocked off by dirt, but I think it comes out somewhere around here where the barn was. We were just starting to look for it."

"Well, now, suppose you just go on looking, boy."

"I can't use the rake with just one hand; it's too heavy. Somebody's got to hold the light so I can see."

The dark figure freed one of Ellen's arms, encircling her waist tightly with the other. "I'll hold it."

Jamie handed him the flashlight. He stared at his mother whose face was still frozen with shock.

"Go on! Get moving!" the voice commanded. He aimed the light around the ash-covered ground. "Start lookin', boy."

Jamie raked the wet ashes from one spot to another until he came to where the grain bin had stood. Then he struck something hard. He knelt to examine his find. After clearing away more ashes, he uncovered a brick panel much like the one he had removed from the chimney. A rusty bolt in the center had crumbled to free the ring Fireplug had found.

"Whatcha got there, boy?" The man dragged Jamie's mother closer. "That the secret panel?"

Jamie stood up. "I think so, but the handle is rusted away. We'll need something to pry it up, and it's too heavy for me. Let my Mom go and do it yourself."

"Don't get smart with me, boy." The man put the flashlight down so that it still shone on the panel. "Hand me that rake."

Still keeping his hold on Jamie's mother, the man began raking. While his attention was diverted, Jamie saw his chance.

With head lowered and hands knotted into fists, he flew at the man's broad back, butting as hard as he could.

Startled, the man let go of Jamie's mother as he tried to regain his balance.

"Run, Mom!" Jamie screamed.

Curses filled the air as the man turned to follow. The rake whistled as it sailed through the air, striking Jamie behind his knees. He fell heavily to the ground and Ellen stopped to help him.

The man was almost upon them when he suddenly stopped in his tracks. His heels dug into the ground.

Elmer had materialized between them in an eerie glow of light. It changed from pale yellow to bright red, and Jamie knew Elmer was seething with anger even though he couldn't see his face.

Relief filled Jamie as he scrambled to his feet. Somehow his pain grew less. He remembered how old Elmer looked like the devil himself when his glow changed to red. His tormentor must really be scared!

"What . . . who . . . who're you?" The voice that came from beneath the sack was shaky now.

A ghostly moan sounded in the night, accompanied by a clanking sound. Jamie saw that Elmer was carrying his chains. A laugh rose in Jamie's throat. The old guy was really making like a ghost with everything he had.

"I am your con-shi-ence . . . your con-shi-ence . . . oooh-oooh-oooh!" Elmer moaned drawing his words out eerily.

The man shrank back. "Go away! Go away!" he stammered, frozen to the spot in fear.

A harsh voice came from within the red glow. "I can't . . . can't . . . can't . ." it wailed. "Not until you confess your sins . . . sins . . . sins . . . oooh-oooh-oooh!" The moan sounded as though it came from a lost soul.

Jamie glanced at his mother. Her eyes were fixed on

the red spectre as though she couldn't believe what she was seeing. He reached for her hand and squeezed it.

"That's Elmer, Mom," he whispered. "Ain't he something?"

The chains made a whistling sound through the air as Elmer swung them over his head, groaning with the effort.

The sound brought the masked man out of his trance. With a gasp, he turned and bolted into the darkness.

"Stop!" Jamie called, but his mother grabbed his arm when he tried to follow.

A car pulled up in the farmyard and headlights flooded the scene. Elmer's glow faded out.

Jamie's father scrambled from the car and came racing toward them with Margaret close behind. "What's going on? Who's out here?" he called. "Ellen . . . is that you! What's wrong?"

She stared at him in shock as though she had never seen him before, and then silently crumpled. He caught her quickly before she hit the ground. "What the . . ." He turned to Jamie. "Son?"

The air grew warmer. Jamie's knees wobbled when he straightened up. "The man who burned our barn came back, Dad. He hurt Mom . . . scared her. Elmer saved us."

"Elmer?"

"The old man I told you about, Dad."

His mother stirred, then groaned. His father held her closer and stared at her with concern etched on his face. "Ellen? Ellen? Are you all right?"

"Mom? Hey, Mom, you okay?" Jamie asked.

Margaret stared at them, eyes wide with fright, unable to speak.

Ellen's eyes opened and she looked around her. "Put me down, Jim. I'm all right."

She took a few tottering steps. "I feel so silly" she muttered, still not completely over her shock. "I don't know what's going on. That weird red light and that spooky old man . . ." Her voice trailed off and she looked around. "Where's that horrible man with the bag on his head?"

"He ran off," Jamie answered.

"*Who* ran off?" his father demanded. "What spooky old man? Will someone please tell me what's going on here?"

Jamie told him what had happened while his father stared in amazement.

"I never should have left you two alone tonight," he said. "Come on, let's get in the house. I'm calling the sheriff. Here, Ellen, take my arm."

Just then another car pulled into the yard and Jamie blinked as the lights flashed in his eyes. Then they were turned off and Sheriff Griffith and a deputy got out.

"Anything wrong, Mr. Boyd?" the sheriff asked.

"Yeah. We were just about to call you," Jim replied. "Our barn burner was back, and this time he attacked my wife as well as Jamie. Come inside and Jamie can tell you about it."

Jamie told the story again. A look of disbelief appeared on the sheriff's face when Jamie came to the part about Elmer, but his mother said she had seen the old man, too. The sheriff nodded, but didn't look convinced.

"Jamie's the bravest boy I know," his mother added. "He tackled that terrible man even though he'd been knocked around by him."

"Are you hurt bad, son?" the sheriff asked.

"Naah, it's okay. I bruise easy, but I heal quick," Jamie answered. A feeling of manhood filled him despite the pain throbbing through his body. For once his parents were proud of him. All through his many scrapes with the law in New York they had stood by him, but he could tell they were ashamed. Now they weren't and it felt nice.

"Can you give me any clue as to the man's identity, Mrs. Boyd?" Sheriff Griffith asked. "Any kind of identification at all, other than that he was big, dressed in black, and wearing a mask."

Jamie's mother shook her head. "It was so dark out there we could hardly see anything."

"Well, I doubt he'll come back tonight," the sheriff said.

"How did you happen to come out here just now?" Jamie's father asked.

The sheriff shook his head. "We're still looking for Dan Carter. Jan's worried sick about him, so a bunch of us decided to form a search party. We found his car in a clump of trees on the back part of your property, Mr. Boyd."

"Could he have been the masked man?"

"Very possible," the sheriff answered. "We'll know when we find him. I posted one of my men by his car in case he tries to drive off."

"You want me to help look?" Jim asked.

The sheriff looked at Jamie and smiled. "I think your family needs you more than we do right now. You folks better lock yourselves in here tonight and try to get some rest. If we haven't found Dan by morning, we may need your help then."

He and his deputy said goodbye and left. Jamie's parents sank into chairs.

"What a night!" his mother said. "Jim, be sure everything is locked tight before we go upstairs."

"Let's go pry up those bricks first, Dad," Jamie said.

"Wha-at?" his father exploded. "Forget it, son! It's way too late!"

"Yes, and I'm going to bed," Margaret said.

"We'd better all turn in, or it'll be time to get up before we're asleep." Ellen smiled at Jamie as the shock of her bad experience that night finally wore off. "Nobody will bother your secret passage tonight, honey, and in the morning we can see what we're doing."

"But, Mom . . ."

"Shush now." She stooped to look under the table. "Fireplug, it's safe to come out."

"Aaah, he wasn't scared of that man, Mom. He just hasn't figured Elmer out yet. Ghosts scare him."

His father groaned. "Ghosts! Masked intruders! What next? Whatever happened to the peace and quiet we came to the country to find? This is getting worse than the city!"

"Never mind, Jim," Ellen said. "After I get Jamie to bed, we can discuss whether to stay here or not."

After his mother tucked Jamie under the covers and gave Fireplug a pat, she closed the door behind her. Sleep was far from Jamie's mind, although he was content to lie on the soft mattress. He thought ahead toward the morning when they would investigate the brick panel in the ground. Would the money be there? Gosh! How would it feel to find ten thousand dollars?

Absent-mindedly, he pulled the cover up to his chin to ward off the sudden chill that filled the room. Then he sat up. When he turned the light on, it didn't surprise him a bit to see Elmer sitting there.

Fireplug's hair stood straight up on end. He tried to burrow underneath the covers, but Jamie grabbed him.

"It's only Elmer, boy. He won't hurt you. Now sit still and stop acting so scared!"

The dog wriggled free and dove under the blankets anyway.

"Doggone it, if he'd just mind *once* in a while, it would be nice," Jamie grumbled.

"Why don't you send him to obedience school?" Elmer asked. "Scooter's dog went, and he does what he's told." Elmer shifted in the chair and groaned. "I think my arthritis is getting worse."

Jamie smiled at the old man. "You sure saved our hides tonight, Elmer. Wow! When you turn red, you really look scary."

"That red glow takes even more out of me than the yellow," Elmer said, letting out a yawn. "Gosh, I'm tired. Why didn't you pull the bag off that feller so we'd know who he was, Jamie? You're not helping me solve this case, you know."

"I started to go after him, but Mom grabbed me," Jamie began, but he corrected himself quickly and looked down. "I didn't think of it. I'm sorry." Then his head rose. "Look, why don't you sleep here tonight?" He moved to the far side of the bed, pushing Fireplug against the wall. "You can have half the bed if you want. I've got enough covers to keep warm."

"I shouldn't, but that sure sounds good," Elmer said. "Thank you. Maybe I *will* snooze in here tonight." He got up from the chair and shuffled over to the bed, groaning as he lowered himself onto it. The old man sighed with pleasure as he stretched out on the mattress.

Jamie's head cocked to one side. The bed hadn't jiggled a bit when Elmer touched it, nor was there any sagging where he lay. Jamie reached out to touch the old man, and again his hand went right through him.

"How can you be here and still not be here?" Jamie asked.

Elmer's eyes opened and he turned to look at Jamie. "Questions, questions," he replied disgustedly. "I'm a ghost, and ghosts can't be touched, I guess."

"Don't you know?"

"Are we gonna sleep or gab?" Elmer asked.

"Why can't I ask about things? You said I should think, and I have to know what I'm thinking about, don't I?"

The old man sighed. "Okay. Ask your questions quick, and then let's knock it off."

"Was the old ring Fireplug brought in the clue you said I'd missed? Is the money in the secret passage?"

"Money! Is that all you think about?" Elmer raised himself on one elbow and frowned at Jamie. "There are lots of things more important in this world than money, you know."

"Well, I want to find it," Jamie insisted. "Is the ring the clue?"

Slowly, Elmer shook his head. "If you ain't the dangdest, most determined boy I ever knew! All right, I'll give you one more hint, and then I ain't gonna say no more. Here it is: when you look ahead and down, don't ever forget to look up, too. Now good night, Jamie." The shaggy head returned to the pillow and a snore bubbled out of Elmer's mouth.

Jamie shivered and pulled the covers up around his

neck. Fireplug was pressed against the small of his back and the warmth from the little dog felt good. The old man needed a place to sleep, but darned if he didn't cool things off when he was around.

He lay thinking about Elmer's words, but they made no sense to him. Jamie buried his nose under the blankets and curled around Fireplug. Morning would come, and then maybe Elmer would tell him more.

CHAPTER TWELVE

"I'VE GOT IT! I'VE GOT IT!"

The sun was shining into the room when Jamie woke. He had dreamed of finding the treasure—stacks of money higher than his head. Almost better than that was not having to go to school today. His mother said she would send a note with Margaret explaining that he had been hurt and asking if he could be excused for another day.

He rolled over to see if Elmer was awake, but there was no one on the other side of the bed. The room was nice and warm. Maybe the old ghost was out looking for the money already.

Jamie dressed and went down to the kitchen. His father looked up.

"Good morning, son. You feeling up to scratch?"

"Sure, Dad. Let's go pry up the brick panel."

"First you eat breakfast," his mother said firmly. "Want some eggs this morning?"

"Just cereal, Mom." Jamie was anxious to get going,

135

and it would be faster to eat corn flakes than waiting for eggs to cook.

Although it took only a few minutes for him to eat, to Jamie it seemed like an hour. His mother put a bowl of meat scraps in front of Fireplug, and from the way he gulped them down, he seemed to be in a hurry, too.

"Let's go, Dad." Jamie said, pushing back his chair.

"You aren't going to leave me behind," his mother said. "After last night and all I went through, I want to see that money, too—if there is any."

His father laughed. "If you believe in ghosts, you surely believe in buried treasure."

"You really don't believe we saw a ghost, do you, Jim? Jamie and I were *there!*"

"I let him have half the bed last night, Mom," Jamie said. "All that glowing wore old Elmer out."

"Okay, you two, let's get on with it." His father brought a long crowbar from the toolroom and carried it outside.

Fireplug raced through the ashes of the old barn and started digging at the bricks.

Jim glanced at him, then shoved the crowbar into the dirt around the bricks and put his weight behind the push. The panel moved, but only one brick popped up.

"The mortar's dry rotted away," he said. "I'll have to pry the bricks loose one at a time and you lift them out, Jamie."

When all the bricks were removed, Jamie peered into the hole they opened. It was shallow. If there ever had been a tunnel, dirt now filled it.

"Aw, gee . . ." Disgust showed on Jamie's face.

His father leaned on the crowbar. "So much for that idea, son. Maybe there *isn't* any money. Looks like that old tunnel's been filled in for a long time."

"All that fuss for nothing," Jamie's mother said. "Well, let's go back to the house and forget about hidden treasure."

Jamie sank back on his heels. He had been so sure there was a tunnel and money hidden inside it. It *must* be around here somewhere. Why else would someone go to such lengths to find it?

"I'm going to start building a chicken coop this morning," his father said. "At least until Sheriff Griffith shows up. I hope they've found Carter. Do you want to help me, son?"

"Sure, Dad . . . only, can Fireplug and me take a walk first?" He wanted to look around some more. Maybe Fireplug would sniff out another hiding place.

"Fresh air will do you good, Jamie. How about another cup of coffee, Ellen? I can sure use one."

Jamie watched his parents walk toward the house, then looked around restlessly. "Find another tunnel, Fireplug . . . or something."

They circled the house and the area where the old barn had stood, but Fireplug stayed beside Jamie. He sniffed bushes and pounced on a cricket. Jamie kicked at clods of dirt. There was nothing that looked like it could be hiding money.

"Come on, boy, let's go see if Mr. Carter's car is still there," he muttered. Fireplug barked and raced ahead of Jamie toward a distant clump of trees.

The sun shone brightly and the smoke from the fire had settled. Jamie smelled the fresh country air, comparing it with the fumes in the streets of New York. A smile tugged at his mouth. He hadn't had a ghost for a companion back there.

What was it Elmer had said? "When you look ahead and down, don't forget to look up, too."

What did he mean? Jamie glanced at the sky. Was he supposed to pray? The old man didn't seem much like a preacher.

Ahead of him Fireplug reached the trees and disappeared into a dip. He growled. The sound floated back to Jamie on the clear morning air. Then Fireplug barked and Jamie broke into a run. When he got to the top of the rise he saw his dog crouched beside a hunting rifle.

"Okay, I see it," Jamie muttered. He stooped to examine the gun. It was polished and clean. Couldn't have been here long. He looked around. Not far away a gully wound through the bottom of the small valley. He went over and looked into it, and his eyes widened in surprise.

At the bottom of the gully a man lay on his back. It was Mr. Carter! One leg was bent sharply at an angle only a broken bone could produce.

Fireplug jumped into the gully, sniffing at the bus driver's still form. Jamie followed him and knelt beside Mr. Carter.

"Mr. Carter! Mr. Carter!" Jamie said. "Oh, gee, are you dead?"

A groan answered him, and then Mr. Carter's eyelids moved. He seemed to have trouble focusing on Jamie.

"Help . . ." he whispered. "Get help . . ." His eyes closed and he lay still.

"Let's go, boy," Jamie said as he jumped up. "We'll get Dad."

He raced back the way he had come with Fireplug bounding ahead of him. When they came in sight of the house, he saw his father.

"Dad! Hey, Dad! We found Mr. Carter!" Jamie called.

His father dropped the tools he was carrying. "What? Where?"

Jamie stopped to catch his breath, then answered, "In a gully. He's hurt. I think he broke his leg."

"Is he alive?"

"Sure, Dad. He talked; said to get help."

His father looked toward the house. "Ellen!" When she opened the door, he shouted, "Call an ambulance and the sheriff! Jamie found Dan Carter and he's hurt!"

She nodded and disappeared, and Jamie's father turned to him. "Show me where he is, son."

They ran to the gully and climbed down beside the fallen man. His eyes were open.

"Carter, what happened?" Jamie's father asked.

"Fell," he mumbled. "Can't move . . . hurts. . ." He groaned. "Couldn't reach my gun . . . thought nobody'd ever come . . ." His eyes closed and his faced winced in pain.

A siren sounded in the distance and Jamie's father got up quickly. "Go show them where we are, son."

"You s'pose he broke his leg running from Elmer last night?" Jamie asked.

His father shook his head. "No. It wasn't him. He's been here longer than that. If that's the ambulance, tell them to get as close as they can and bring a stretcher. Hurry, Jamie."

Jamie climbed out of the gully and went to where he could see the ambulance pulling into the farmyard. He waved both arms and the driver veered toward him. Two men in white uniforms climbed out when it stopped. One of them grabbed a box of first aid equipment from the front seat next to him, and the other asked Jamie where they should go.

"Down in the gully," Jamie answered. "Dad said you'll need a stretcher. He can't move much."

They opened the back of the ambulance and lifted a wheeled bed out. "This is what they call a gurney, son," one of the men said. "Lead the way."

Jamie led them to the gully.

"Down here, men," his father called.

The men climbed down and knelt beside Carter, checking him over thoroughly. After determining where the break occurred in the leg, they carefully slid a board under the groaning man and lifted him gently onto the gurney. They covered him with a blanket and rolled him up to the edge of the gully.

"He'll be all right once we get him to the hospital," one of the men said. "You probably saved his life. That leg looks bad."

"My son found him," Jamie's father said.

"Fireplug found his gun," Jamie added.

They formed a procession to the ambulance. When Carter was safely inside, the driver steered slowly across the field to the road.

Sheriff Griffith's car turned into the lane. It met the ambulance and both vehicles paused. Jamie could see the sheriff talking to the driver. Then the ambulance sped off toward the hospital. The sheriff drove up to the house and stopped. He got out and waited until Jamie and his father reached him.

"I see you found Dan Carter," he said.

Jamie's father told him what happened and the sheriff nodded.

"Jamie, if this keeps up I'm going to have to hire you as a deputy," the sheriff said. "My men searched all night and couldn't find him. You and your dog did a good job."

"Dad says he couldn't be the man that grabbed Mom last night," Jamie said.

"Probably not," the sheriff agreed. "I'll go tell Jan we found her father. Then I'm taking that knife to the hospital to ask Dan if he knows whose it is. He's been carving with other whittlers since he was a boy. Maybe he can identify it." He paused. "You find any money yet?"

Jamie shook his head in disappointment. "That old tunnel was full of dirt."

"Well, don't feel bad, Jamie. I never did think there was any money buried out here. Anyway, I'll let you all know what I find out," the sheriff said, making his way back to his car.

After the sheriff had driven away, Jamie's father picked up the tools he had dropped when Jamie first called to him. "Guess I can get back to building that chicken coop now. Want to help?"

"Sure."

"Maybe your ghost will do the heavy part."

Jamie looked around. Was Elmer out Here somewhere?

Where could you look down, ahead, then up, and find something that had been hidden? Jamie saw the house in front of them, and the brick chimney with its old escape tunnel.

"I've got it!" he shouted suddenly. "Hey, Dad . . . *I've got it!*"

CHAPTER THIRTEEN

"COUNT IT, JAMIE"

"Got what, son? What are you talking about?"

Jamie headed for the house. "Come on, Dad!" was all he said, tugging his father lightly by the arm.

His father followed him. As they got inside, Jamie said, "Mom, come on! I know where the money is hidden!"

He raced through the kitchen to the hall and up the stairs. His parents kept asking questions as they followed, but Jamie was too excited to answer them. Fireplug yipped with excitement, almost tripping Jamie as he darted between his feet.

Jamie yanked open the door to the third floor and ran up the steps, his aches forgotten. He heard his father following close behind him, still asking questions. If Elmer said what Jamie thought he had said, the money would soon be found.

Fireplug whimpered when Jamie climbed the ladder to the attic. His father ordered the dog to sit and followed

Jamie up the rungs.

At the top, he turned and looked down through the trap door. "Come on, Ellen, I'll give you a hand. I don't know where we're going, but I think you'd better come along."

"I wouldn't miss it," she said. "Where's Jamie?"

Jamie raced over to the chimney and poked his head into the gaping hole. He looked down, then up. Faint daylight shone through the chimney top, but hardly enough to see anything in the blackened enclosure. He reached up, carefully feeling the hook where the old rope had hung. His fingers traced its outline, then moved onward. Only caked soot rewarded his effort.

He turned to the other side of the opening and felt another iron hook. A leather bag hung from it. Jamie lifted it from the hook and pulled it out through the opening in the chimney.

"See?" he announced triumphantly, displaying his find to his parents. His fingers fumbled with the drawstring for suspenseful seconds before the pouch finally came open. Inside were bills—lots of them!

"It's here!" Jamie crowed, jumping up and down excitedly. "I found the money!"

"Oh, my," his mother said in a faint voice, sinking down weakly on one of the rusty old cots. "There really *is* money!"

"And lots of it, from the look of things," Jim said. "Count it, Jamie."

Jamie began counting the money, piling it into neat stacks on a big box. It was all in large bills—fifties and one hundreds—and the counting went quickly. He was laughing when he finished, and his eyes shone with joy.

"Oh, boy!" he cried. "We've got eleven stacks with a

thousand dollars in each of 'em, and four hundred dollars besides! Mom! Dad! We're *rich*!"

"Not yet, son," Jim cautioned. "We'd better find out if it's ours first. Put it all back in the bag and we'll take it to Sheriff Griffith. We can't let this go unreported."

Jim picked up the leather bag and handed it to Jamie. The boy's face took on a look of disappointment.

"But the sheriff said it was finder's keepers," Jamie said.

"*Only* if no one else has a legal claim to it," his father reminded him. "Come on, son, we have to report this. People who obey the law sleep better at night."

"Maybe we should wait until tomorrow, Jim," Jamie's mother said. "The sheriff will be at the hospital with Mr. Carter, and he'll want to talk to him before he does anything else. Besides, someone should be here when Margaret gets home—and I certainly don't want to wait by myself. That terrible man might still be prowling around!"

She shuddered as the frightening experience of the night before flashed back to her.

"Of course I won't leave any of you by yourselves until he's found," Jamie's father answered. He shrugged. "Well, Jamie, guess we might as well start on the chicken coop. Put that bag of money in your room where it'll be safe."

Jamie carried the pouch to his room, his mind spinning with thoughts. He had never seen so much money before! Just think of the things it would buy! He looked around, wondering where to hide it. This old house was so creaky, you never knew who could be walking around in it. He decided his bed would be the best place, and stuffed the bag of money under the mattress.

"We'll sleep on it, Fireplug. That way nobody can steal it without us knowing!"

While he helped his father with the carpentry, they talked about the money and tried to guess the identity of the prowler. Midway through the afternoon Jamie looked up to see Chuck Magruder coming down the road.

"Look, Dad." Jamie pointed.

"It's the boy you had the fight with," his father said. "Well, maybe he's come to make up for it."

"More likely he wants to start another fight," Jamie muttered.

"Now why would he do that? Go up to him and make friends. Go on. Shake hands and forget all that fighting business."

Jamie nodded in agreement. "Hi," his father called as Chuck got closer.

Chuck walked over to where they were working. "Hi, Mr. Boyd . . . Jamie."

"Whatcha want?" Jamie asked suspiciously. "How come you ain't in school?"

"Aw, I've been sick again. I just thought I'd walk over and see how you're doing. We can be friends, can't we?" He tossed a ball into the air. "Want to play catch?"

"Go ahead, Jamie," his father said. "We've worked enough for today."

The two boys walked a short distance away and exchanged a few words. Jim watched as they shook hands and moved apart to begin playing catch.

Jamie caught the ball Chuck threw him. Hey, maybe old Chuck wasn't so bad after all. He didn't act like he wanted to fight anymore. Jamie threw the ball back.

"See your old ghost lately?" Chuck asked.

"Yeah," Jamie replied.

"Find any money yet?"

"Uh huh. We're taking it to the sheriff tomorrow."

"Wow! That's great!" Chuck cried. "Where'd you find it?"

"I can't tell you. Not until we report it to the sheriff," Jamie answered.

Jamie waited to catch the ball, but Chuck didn't throw it. "Well, we gonna play or not?" he asked.

Chuck shook his head. "I just remembered something I have to do at home before it gets too late. Sorry. See you tomorrow, Jamie."

Jamie said goodbye and watched him leave, then went to the house. It was time for Margaret to get home and then they'd eat supper. He was hungry. Besides, he was anxious for tomorrow to arrive. Would the sheriff let them keep the money? He sure hoped so.

When Margaret got home Jamie told her about the money and, of course, she insisted on seeing it. Jamie brought it out from under the mattress to show her.

"Wow!" she gasped. "Can I get some new dresses now?"

Her mother laughed. "Let's not plan how to spend it before we know it's ours to keep."

The evening passed slowly. Finally it was time for Jamie to go to bed. He lay in the darkness, too excited to sleep, and listened to the rest of the family going to their rooms. The house quieted, and Jamie was still lying wide-eyed and fully awake. He thought about motor scooters and ponies and all the other nice things money can buy. Then he closed his eyes and tried to will himself to sleep. The old house creaked as the air outside grew cold. Where *was* Elmer tonight? He would sure like to tell him about the money.

At last he dozed off, but nightmares troubled his sleep. Jamie tossed fitfully while a hazy black dragon chased him through his dreams. Finally, with a lunge, the dragon caught him. Jamie fought to open his eyes and stared up at a dark form bending over him. A hand clamped over his mouth.

"Where's the money?" a harsh voice demanded. A knife glistened above him. "If you yell when I take my hand away, I'll kill you!"

The hand left his mouth and Jamie swallowed the lump of fear that welled up in his throat.

"Well? You gonna talk?" He brought the knife against Jamie's throat.

Where was Fireplug? He should be barking like crazy. "What'd you do to my dog?" Jamie demanded.

"I took care of him first. Now, where's the money?" the intruder snarled. The knife was still at Jamie's throat.

A cold gust of air chilled the room.

Jamie pushed the knife away and felt it cut into his hand. A powerful backhand slammed into his face.

"You ain't got no sense at all, do you boy!" the man hissed. The knife was back at Jamie's neck and a rough hand held him down.

"You killed my dog!"

"Not yet, I didn't. Just whacked him cold. But I'll go back and finish the job if you don't tell me where you hid that money!."

Jamie's hand stung and he could feel blood trickling from the cut. His ears rang from the blow he received.

Fireplug! He couldn't let old Fireplug get killed over some money! "It's under the mattress," he muttered.

The intruder held Jamie with one hand while he felt under the mattress with the other. Where had he put the knife? Jamie wondered, scheming to get the weapon away from the man. He tried to break free, but the grip on his arm tightened.

"Here it is!" the man announced, pulling the bag out.

Suddenly, a glow filled the room and Jamie saw Elmer in its midst. The intruder stiffened. The pouch dropped from his hand, and he stared open-mouthed at the eerie sight.

Thinking quickly, Jamie reached up and pulled the sack off the man's head. "This is him, Elmer! See?"

"Who-oo-oo-oo are you-oo-oo-oo?" Elmer moaned.

The man shrank back, stammering words no one could understand.

Elmer moaned again. He filled his cheeks and blew a gust of cold air over the man. White rime covered him and an icicle formed at the end of his nose. The intruder shuddered.

"Tell-ll-ll me you-oo-oo-or na-aa-ame or I'll free-ee-eeze you solid!" Elmer roared.

The dark-faced man's eyes were wide with fright. His whole body trembled. "C-c-caleb M-m-magruder," he stuttered.

"You're Chuck's father!" Jamie exclaimed. "*You* killed old Mathieson!" He grabbed the pouch of money where it had fallen on the bed.

Magruder glanced fearfully from Jamie to the old ghost. He tried to back farther away, but the wall prevented him from retreating.

The glow was bright red now and Elmer's face was terrifying as his anger grew. "Confess!" he thundered. "I'll haunt you-oo-oo forev-v-ver if you-oo-oo don't!"

Magruder tried to brush away the ice from his nose, but it was stuck there. "I didn't mean to," he whispered. "I didn't *mean* to do it!"

A door slammed and footsteps were heard scurrying down the hall. Elmer's glow had faded, but his voice sounded in the darkness. "Caleb Magruder, confess what you've done or I'll be back!" he warned. Another cold blast of air filled the room.

The door flew open and the light went on. Jamie's father stood in the doorway. "Who are you?" he demanded.

Magruder was still cowering in fright, face buried in his hands. "Caleb Magruder," he whimpered. "I killed old Mathieson! It was an accident! I didn't mean to! He owed me money and wouldn't pay up, even though he got enough when he sold that property." The words were muffled but clear as they came from beneath his hands.

"Jamie, are you all right?" his mother asked as she came in. "Oh my gosh! You're cut!" Her glance went to Fireplug lying motionless on the floor. "Your dog! What happened?"

Jamie jumped out of bed and crouched over Fireplug. He examined the little body to see if anything was broken. "Wake up, boy! Fireplug, wake up!"

"What's happening?" Margaret asked, pulling a robe tighter around her.

"Go phone the sheriff Margaret," her father said, racing over to scoop up Magruder's knife. "Ellen, you take care of Jamie. All right, Magruder," he continued, grasping the knife firmly. "You won't be needing this anymore." He motioned him out of the room.

Magruder meekly obeyed and Jim marched him downstairs, guarding him closely.

"Oh, Jamie, you're hurt again," his mother said, walking over to him. "I'd better get the antiseptic. And bandages." She hurried out.

Jamie picked Fireplug up in his arms, and cradled him gently. The pouch of money was forgotten. The little dog lay so still; Jamie had never seen him this quiet before. "Don't die," he whispered. "Please don't die!"

The room had grown warmer, but still Fireplug didn't move. Tears filled Jamie's eyes. He couldn't go on without his dog! He just couldn't. His eyes fell on the pouch of money. He'd give every cent in that pouch if it would help old Fireplug.

Suddenly the small body stirred. Fireplug's eyes opened and he shook his head. Jamie bent over him and a red tongue licked at his nose. Fireplug wiggled free and jumped down, shaking himself all over. He staggered and fell back against Jamie.

"You okay, boy?"

Fireplug regained his balance. His tail wagged. He barked and looked up at Jamie.

"You're okay! Oh, Fireplug, you're okay!"

Jamie's mother returned with a basin of water and an armful of supplies. "But you aren't," she said. "Let me see that hand."

Jamie picked up his dog and sat on the edge of the bed. "He's not hurt bad, Mom." He let her dunk his hand into the basin and dry it. The antiseptic smarted, but he was so happy about his dog he didn't mind. When he was bandaged, his mother said she had better get down to the kitchen.

"I'll go with you, Mom. We caught Mr. Mathieson's killer."

"We?"

"Elmer and me. He kept Mr. Magruder from slitting my throat."

His mother shuddered. "Oh, dear! How can these things keep happening to us?"

"I guess we're just lucky, Mom." Jamie shoved the pouch of money back under the mattress, then followed his mother down the stairs.

In the kitchen Caleb Magruder was slumped over the table, his shoulders bowed. Margaret had put the teakettle on to heat. Jim stood guard over the beaten man.

"You have a lot to answer for, Magruder," he said quietly.

A car pulled up outside, its lights gleaming through the windows before they were turned off. Sheriff Griffith and a deputy came running to the door, entering without knocking.

"You're under arrest, Magruder!" the sheriff announced, walking over to him and placing the handcuffs around his wrists. He then read Magruder his rights.

"He confessed to Mathieson's murder," Jamie's father said. "Or rather, the killing. He said it was accidental."

"Yeah, but he threatened to kill Fireplug," Jamie added. "Me, too. Said he'd slit my throat if I didn't tell where the money was."

"Well, it seems we've got plenty to charge you with, Magruder," the sheriff said. "Dan Carter recognized the knife Jamie found, and it appears to be yours." He took a second look at Jamie. "You banged up some more? My gosh!'"

"Jamie gets the credit for capturing Magruder and getting a confession out of him," his father said,

"And Elmer," Jamie added. The old guy was right. A man should think things out for himself, and from now on Jamie would. It was sort of nice to be a hero instead of being lectured for doing something wrong.

The sheriff talked with Jamie's parents and Jamie noticed he had ignored his mention of Elmer. The sheriff probably didn't know what to think about Jamie's claim to seeing a ghost. After all, he hadn't seen him. Well, at least his mother had.

After the sheriff's deputy had taken Magruder out to the patrol car, the sheriff turned to Jamie. "I forgot to bring a badge again, Jamie, but it's just as well. Instead of being just a make-believe deputy, how'd you like to be one of my *real* deputies? Without pay, of course," he added, smiling, "and not wearing a gun just yet."

Jamie considered the matter and then slowly shook his head. "I don't think so," he said with a grin. "Maybe later, when I get a little bigger."

"He's right," his father agreed. "Making him a deputy now would just make trouble with the other boys. We'll be in to see you tomorrow. We need to talk to you about the money."

"You found it?"

Jamie's father nodded. "Yes, in all this confusion, I forgot to mention it earlier. Jamie found it. Magruder was trying to take it away from him when we caught him."

Sheriff Griffith shook his head. "I would never have believed it! How much was there?"

"Eleven thousand four hundred dollars!" Jamie said.

"My goodness! So all along the rumors were true. Keep it in a safe place and bring it in to me tomorrow. I'll check and see if there are any other claims against it."

At the door he paused. "I'd never have believed it," he repeated.

When he had gone, Margaret put cups on the table. "Anybody want tea?"

Her father sat down. "I really need something stronger after all this, but I guess tea will do."

His eyes met Ellen's. "Why us?" he continued, shaking his head. "Why did we ever buy this place?"

Jamie's mother laughed. "Because it's a nice place, Jim. And now that the killer and the money have been found, maybe things will quiet down."

"Elmer will leave!" Jamie cried out.

Jamie's parents and Margaret stared at him.

"He'll leave now," Jamie insisted. "The case is solved and old Elmer can go home. Gee, Mom . . . I'll miss him!"

"I'd sure like to see this ghost of yours," his father said. "Somehow I feel like I'm missing out on something."

"I don't think you ever will, Dad. But Mom saw him, didn't you, Mom?"

"I saw him," she agreed. "Let's finish our tea and try to get some sleep, Jim. I'll describe Elmer in detail for you tomorrow. *Again.*"

When they had settled themselves in for the remainder of the night, Jamie stared into the darkness of his room. "Elmer? Elmer, you here?" he called.

There was no answer. No other sound. No gust of icy air came to answer Jamie. A forlorn feeling came over him. Had Elmer gone without saying good bye?

CHAPTER FOURTEEN

"LOOK AT THAT RAINBOW!"

The next morning Jamie and his parents got ready to take the money into town.

"Don't I belong to this family?" Margaret asked. "Why do I have to go to school when so much is happening?"

"So at least one of my children will be educated," her mother answered. "This is the last day for Jamie to miss. Once we get this money matter settled, it's school for *both* of you."

"Well, I hope Mr. Carter gets well soon so he can drive our bus," Margaret said. "We get jerked all over the place with that new driver."

"It'll take awhile for his leg to heal," her mother said. "In the meantime, your new driver will improve. Driving a bus is hard. We'll be here when you get home this afternoon."

"Well, with our barn burner in jail, we should be able to live without all this fear," her father said. "But like

155

your mother said, we'll be here when you get home."

Jamie held the bag of money while he sat in the front seat between his mother and father on the short ride to town. He wondered about the money, but somehow it didn't seem quite so important now. He had been willing to give it all up to save Fireplug. A dog was something a guy just couldn't do without.

Obedience school for Fireplug would probably cost a lot of money, but that was one thing Jamie wanted for sure. He wanted to be as proud of Fireplug as Scooter was of O'Brien of County Cork. Besides, if he could get his dog to mind, Fireplug could be saved a lot of trouble in the future.

Sheriff Griffith was in his office when they arrived. The whole inside could be seen through the front plate glass window. It looked like the other buildings on Main Street and had probably been a store at one time.

The sheriff glanced up, then got to his feet when Jamie and his parents walked in. "Good morning, folks. I was just thinking about you. Now that Magruder is behind bars, you can relax and see that we aren't usually so violent in this county."

"Let's hope things get peaceful," Jamie's father said, smiling at Jamie. "We came here to find peace and quiet, not killers and barn burners."

"You will," the sheriff said. "You'll have your peace and quiet now."

"We brought the money in," Jamie said, holding out the leather bag. "Over eleven thousand dollars!"

"Imagine that!" The sheriff sat down. "I thought the whole thing was so much hogwash."

"No, sir. There was a real ghost out there, too," Jamie

said.

"Maybe we'd better leave Elmer out of this," his mother said quickly. "Let's just say we found a new friend—an old man who dropped in for a visit, sheriff. He *is* a little ghostlike, but quite real."

"Oh." The sheriff cocked an eyebrow at Jamie. "You youngsters like to put us on, don't you? Well, I'm glad you found some money, and I hope you use it to good advantage."

"Is it ours to keep?"

"It was in your chimney, wasn't it? Your dad bought the farm—lock, stock and barrel, didn't he?" Sheriff Griffith nodded. "I'd say it was yours—except for the taxes you'll have to pay on it."

"What about Magruder?" Jamie's father asked.

"Well . . . he'll have to stand trial, that's for sure. I feel sorry for Mrs. Magruder. She's a nice old soul, and all this has been a shock to her. She's the one who will suffer, what with the expense of a lawyer and such. Might even have to sell their farm."

"Did Mathieson really owe them money?"

"Yes, he did, Mr. Boyd. Mrs. Magruder said they had foolishly loaned the Mathiesons five thousand dollars and didn't get a note for it. Mrs. Mathieson was her cousin. She promised to pay the money back as soon as they sold that other property. Then Magruder and the old man got into some kind of argument and Mathieson got stubborn." The sheriff shook his head. "Folks just don't realize how much trouble they can make for themselves."

Jamie listened to them talk and his eyes strayed to the money he was holding. You needed money to buy the things you wanted, but maybe you didn't need all that much. He was thinking about this when he suddenly realized the conversation had stopped. He looked up and met his father's eyes.

"What are you thinking about, son?"

"Oh. . . the money I found. It's a lot, isn't it?"

"Sure is."

"And we can keep it all?"

His father nodded. "We bought it with the farm."

Jamie sat in thought. Suddenly a finger of ice touched his nose and left a thin coating of rime. He wiped it away with his sleeve. He saw his mother watching him and smiled at her. "Guess we bought a lot of things with the farm."

She laughed. "Guess we did, honey. Including a lot of *trouble.*"

"Well, if old Mathieson's money is ours, probably what he owes is, too. Dad? You think we should give Mrs. Magruder part of this?"

His father nodded. "I do, son."

Jamie handed the bag to the sheriff. "Take out what's hers."

The sheriff took the bag, counted out five thousand dollars and handed the rest back to Jamie.

The door to the sheriff's office opened by itself. Everyone looked as the door swung wide. Then it closed, gently, and the latch clicked in the silence.

"Now what caused that?" Sheriff Griffith asked.

"Perhaps the wind is coming up," Jamie's mother said.

When the Boyds completed their business in the sheriff's office, they climbed into their car for the ride home.

"That was a generous thing to do, Jamie," his father said quietly. "We're all very proud of you."

"Well, you gotta be fair, don't you, Dad?"

"You sure do son. You've just learned a very important lesson."

"Look at that rainbow!" his mother exclaimed, pointing to eastern sky. "How can there be a rainbow when it hasn't been raining?"

Jamie looked through the window ahead. A multicolored ribbon arched almost directly over them like a bridge between land and sky. It had a glitter like no rainbow Jamie had ever seen.

"Isn't it beautiful?" his mother asked.

"It sure is odd," his father muttered.

Jamie laughed. "Elmer was so far over-the-hill, I bet he couldn't make it home without a ladder. High as that one is, I'll bet his feet are hurting."

"Elmer . . . Elmer . . . how come I didn't see this ghost you two keep talking about?" Jamie's father asked.

"Perhaps you didn't need him as much as Jamie and I did, Jim," Ellen replied.

"You s'pose he'll ever come back, Mom?"

"Maybe," his mother said softly. "You have to keep an open mind about these things, you know."

Jamie nodded. That you did!